WHITMAN

SEVEN GREAT DETECTIVE STORIES

Edited by William H. Larson

Illustrated by Michael Lowenbein

A WHITMAN BOOK
Western Publishing Company, Inc.
Racine, Wisconsin

• • • • • ACKNOWLEDGMENTS • • • • •

"Suspect Unknown" by Courtney Ryley Cooper. Reprinted by permission of Mrs. Courtney Ryley Cooper. This story first appeared in ELLERY QUEEN'S MYSTERY MAGAZINE.

"The Nine-Mile Walk" by Harry Kemelman. Copyright 1947 by The American Mercury, Inc. This story first appeared in ELLERY QUEEN'S MYSTERY MAGAZINE, and is reprinted by permission of the author and his agents: Scott Meredith Literary Agency, Inc., 580 Fifth Avenue, New York, New York 10036.

"The Missing Undergraduate" by Henry Wade. Reprinted by permission of A. D. Peters & Co.

"Silver Blaze" by Arthur Conan Doyle. Reprinted by permission of the Estate of Sir Arthur Conan Doyle.

"The Blast of the Book," from THE SCANDAL OF FATHER BROWN by G. K. Chesterton. Copyright 1933, 1935 by G. K. Chesterton. Copyright renewed 1963 by Oliver Chesterton. Reprinted by permission of Dodd, Mead & Company, Inc., Miss D. E. Collins, and Cassell & Co. Ltd.

"The Man in the Velvet Hat" by Jerome and Harold Prince. Reprinted by permission of the authors. This story first appeared in ELLERY QUEEN'S MYSTERY MAGAZINE.

Library of Congress Catalog Card Number: 68-25323

0-307-01627-7

CONTENTS

AN INTRODUCTION

"Pardon me, sir," quoth the detective-story writer. "I have a little murder here, and I wonder if you'd care to come along and help try to solve it. Perhaps you'll be able to find the answer even before the inspector does. . . ."

Thus the chronicler of the Great Detective issues his invitation to the reader. It is an invitation which has been issued countless millions of times, from the World War II bomb shelters of London to the favorite easy chair of Mr. Joe Average, seeking to while away a quiet evening. And the invitation will continue to be accepted—most heartily, thank you—because the detective story will continue to give the reader what he wants: an intriguing puzzle of sufficient complexity to make him feel truly involved in its unraveling.

The stories in this book carry the same invitation. You will find them varied enough to suit most tastes, we trust.

"Suspect Unknown" by Courtney Ryley Cooper is a classic story of the FBI written by a man whose knowledge of crime-detection techniques led to having many of his stories endorsed by the FBI. That the author ran away from home at the age of sixteen to become a circus clown and later served as press agent for "Buffalo Bill" Cody only serves to further whet one's curiosity about this multi-faceted man.

"The Blast of the Book" introduces to the reader G. K. Chesterton's beloved Father Brown, who combines the roles of priest and detective, a rather unlikely combination, to say the least.

Henry Wade's "The Missing Undergraduate" brings Detective-Inspector John Poole, of Scotland Yard, back to his Oxford alma mater to help locate a missing student—who is eventually located, but under extremely peculiar circumstances.

Jacques Futrelle's unlikely detective, The Thinking Machine, is featured in "The Problem of Cell 13," one of the earliest—and best—variations on the locked-room puzzle so dear to the hearts of writers in the past. The Thinking Machine is dedicated to the proposition that "two plus two equals four, not *some* of the time but *all* of the time."

Sir Arthur Conan Doyle's "Silver Blaze" presents that master of detection, the incomparable Sherlock Holmes, with a perplexing puzzle in horsemanship. Holmes, one of the most imitated figures in literature, certainly needs no further introduction.

In "The Nine-Mile Walk" by Harry Kemelman the

10

reader encounters a problem in logic, a mental exercise in drawing inferences that leads to an astounding conclusion.

Our last selection, "The Man in the Velvet Hat" by Jerome and Harold Prince, injects something of the supernatural into a detective story, as the ubiquitous Man in the Velvet Hat holds our nation's largest city in terror.

"You say you thought it was the butler? Tsk-tsk. You should have noted that he had neither motive nor opportunity. When Lady Penelope discovered the body in the den. . . ."

We shall let the authors explain.

WILLIAM H. LARSON

SUSPECT UNKNOWN

Courtney Ryley Cooper

INSPECTOR JESSUP of the Washington Field Office of the Federal Bureau of Investigation had been expecting the call. He smiled slightly as he listened to the telephone report:

"Agent Benson speaking from the first floor. The subject just got out of his car as a sight-seeing bus arrived for a tour of the bureau. He immediately mingled with a bunch of sightseers and is headed upstairs on one of the first elevator loads. Agent Torner is trailing him, subject to your orders, sir."

"Rejoin Agent Torner and continue the surveillance," commanded the inspector and hung up. A big man, sandy-haired, pleasant-featured, he shifted in his chair with a certain air of lumbering boyishness and eyed for an instant the intercommunicating system. For once he could give thanks that he was head of the Washington office.

At other times he had been not too delighted with

13

his assignment. This was a "spot" job, constantly under the eye of the director; the distance between Inspector Jessup's office and the nerve center of the entire FBI was only the difference between the fourth and fifth floors of the big marble building of the United States Department of Justice. Under ordinary conditions the proximity meant that the inspector's activities were subject to far greater scrutiny than those of any other like officer in the organization. But at a time like this. . . .

He flipped a button on the interoffice system, marked "Director." Instantly a crisp voice answered, "Yes, Jessup."

The inspector leaned close to the transmitter.

"Hello, Boss. The suspect in the Tilliver murder case just came into the building for another tour of the bureau."

"Good! That makes the third trip in three days."

"And that either makes me dead right on him or dead wrong. He must figure he's got that job covered up pretty well and wants to be sure of it. After all, once he leaves Washington he can't run and hide like the average fugitive. He's a prominent man. He's got to stay in the open, and that takes a lot of nerve— unless a person knows that there isn't a chance of being caught. So what happens? He remembers his crook training: to stick in with officers after a crime and try to hear or see something that will tip him off as to how they're progressing with the case. That's my theory—I'll stand or fall on it."

"All right, Jessup. Go ahead with your plans."

"On the lines we talked over yesterday afternoon?"

14

"Definitely."

"There's a point, Boss. To do that, I'll have to divulge a certain amount of information about the case. How far shall I go?"

There was a pause. Then: "That's up to your judgment, Jessup. Your job is to place him actually at the scene of the crime. If you can do that, all our other evidence dovetails. We know he was seen in the neighborhood both before and after the murder. The witnesses we had hidden here yesterday when he went through were fairly certain on that point. We know, too, that Tilliver and a man who looked a lot like this fellow served a term in California together some twenty years ago on a charge of extortion by mail."

"But there's no fingerprint record to prove it."

"That's the tough part; the fingerprint files on that prison don't date back that far. So you've got to work carefully. As I see it, you figure that he and Tilliver were once crooked pals. After they got out of prison they went different ways. Tilliver seemingly reformed. So did this fellow. You believe that neither of them did anything of the sort. Tilliver was still a blackmailer at heart, and this—what's his name?"

"Manton Kent."

"That's right—Kent. This Kent got into a small concern—handling all sorts of things—and apparently built it up to a big business—"

"But we can show by evidence that it's a house of cards. That's my idea of the motive, Boss. On the surface, it looks as if he killed Tilliver rather than pay him blackmail. But I think he did it because he figured that Tilliver knew what Kent was doing in this firm—

juggling its stock, selling off its assets for his personal account, padding payrolls. . . . It'll take a dozen auditors to chase down the crooked things this fellow's done. Tilliver must have found this out, tried to get some blackmail as a result of what he knew—but got killed instead."

"It's a great theory—if you can prove it."

Inspector Jessup's lips tightened.

"Yes, that's the trouble—to prove it. To put him smack into the middle of the murder scene, or get some sort of record on him through fingerprints."

"There were none at the scene of the crime."

"And no record from the penitentiary. I didn't mean that. I was hoping that I might find he'd served time somewhere else. Or been arrested for investigation, or mixed up in some bankrupt racket—anything to break through his armor. Otherwise, I haven't a leg to stand on."

"Especially since all the tangible evidence points directly away from him. Well, use your head on that, Jessup. And good luck to you."

A clicking sound was followed by silence. Inspector Jessup raised a big hand to his forehead and brought it away, the palm beaded with sweat. He wished now that he had not been so eager to work personally on the solution of this murder, that he had not been so enthusiastic in the belief that Manton Kent, following a crook's logic, was attempting to spy on those who were spying on him.

Suddenly, however, he straightened. In quick succession, he flipped the levers of the interoffice system to a half dozen departments and gave crisp orders.

Then he glanced at his watch. It was twelve minutes past ten o'clock. The morning tour of the building had begun promptly at ten. By now, the inspector knew, the guide had explained the wide-flung activities of the bureau; he should be completing the tour's beginning in the exhibit room with a few words on the machine guns captured from gangsters; Dillinger's death mask; the red wig worn by Katherine Kelly, the kidnapper; and the vacuum jar in which her husband had hidden ransom money. The inspector pressed a button. A special agent answered.

"I'll begin at the multigraphing room," said Inspector Jessup. "See that someone is always accidentally available if I should need him."

"Yes, sir."

The inspector left the room. After a time, special agents followed. It was five minutes later that, crowding and gawking, the morning tour of Department of Justice sightseers followed their FBI guide down a wide hall on the seventh floor toward a long room where presses whirred, multigraphs pounded noisily, and binding machinery clattered. The guide entered the door, walking backward that he might address the variegated group that had followed him. Here were men and women from throughout America who tonight would send home postcards saying they knew all about crime. There were small boys and girls, goggle-eyed at the thought of being in the same building with G-men. There was a sprinkling of newspapermen and women from out of town, and not a few who appeared to be business executives or persons of responsibility interested in law enforcement. At one side, somewhat apart from the throng, was a keen-featured man of about forty-five who bore a frank air of interest in everything about him. The guide, still walking backward, now raised his voice above the roar of machinery.

"In this room," he began, "are all the reproductive processes by which reward sheets are multigraphed, pamphlets bound, and the FBI's Law Enforcement Bulletin assembled and shipped to more than ten thousand police bodies, sheriffs, and other enforcement agencies. In a kidnapping, the lists of ransom notes are reproduced here; in one case, this room turned out a job in thirty-six hours of continuous effort that would have required three weeks of work in a regulation printing plant. Now, if you will follow me—"

"Look out!" came a sharp voice. The warning was too late. The guide collided heavily with the hurrying form of Inspector Jessup, striking him against an elbow. The inspector winced; his right hand flew open, releasing a number of sheets of paper that evidently had just come from a multigraphing machine and scattering them wildly across the smooth cement floor.

"That's all right; that's all right!" the inspector announced hastily to the guide's apologies, bending swiftly, meanwhile, in an effort to gather up the papers. Here and there a visitor, seeking to aid, bent also. The inspector apparently took no notice. His eyes, however, were not still.

At last he saw that the keen-eyed man, also a volunteer in the job of reclamation, was covertly peering at each sheet as he picked it from the floor. The inspector

18

waited only a moment more, then, as with sudden realization, whirled.

"Please don't touch those papers, anyone!" he commanded. A passing agent suddenly moved in upon the scene, joining with the guide in collecting the multigraphed matter from the hands of volunteers. The inspector nodded to the guide.

"If you will move on with your party."

"Yes, sir. Please follow me." The group obeyed, and the inspector stood facing the subject of his investigation, who stood extending a sheaf of the papers with one hand, while with the other he fumbled at a hip pocket for his wallet.

"I'm afraid that my curiosity got the better of me," he announced. "I was so terribly interested that I did not realize this might be a confidential matter."

The inspector's brow creased.

"You mean you were reading that announcement?"

"I glanced at it." His hands now free, he dug into his wallet for a card. "I do hope that my position will guarantee my ability to keep secrets. Kent is my name, sir. Manton Kent. I am president of Superior Products."

The inspector lost his worried look, extending a pawlike hand in greeting. The main group had passed out of the room now. The guide's voice echoed from down the hall: "We are now entering the identification unit, where are assembled a total of more than ten million fingerprints from every part of the United States and numerous foreign countries—"

"I suppose I should catch up with that group," said Manton Kent. "Although," he laughed, "I almost know that lecture by heart."

"Oh, you've been here before?"

"This is my third trip in three days."

"Interested in law enforcement?"

Manton Kent smiled.

"I didn't realize it until I came through here the other day. Then I began to see how many features could be applied to my business. Fingerprinting, for instance, and scientific apparatus. Although, of course," he added slowly, "one only gets the barest sort of a glimpse on one of these tours."

The inspector agreed.

"I'm sorry you didn't make yourself known at the director's office. He'd have arranged for a special guide."

"You really think so?"

"Oh, yes. Persons like yourself, heads of corporations and the like, are the real ones he wants interested in the things we are doing here."

Manton Kent shrugged.

"So what do I do? I play the boob and look at what turns out to be a confidential matter."

Inspector Jessup grinned.

"Oh, it isn't that bad. Fact is, what's on this sheet is not so terribly secret."

"I'm glad of that."

"It's a bureau matter, of course. Naturally we don't want any investigative information to fall into the wrong hands. This just happens to be some multigraphs of reports on evidence we've picked up in a murder case here in Washington a few days ago. A man named James Tilliver was killed in his home. Ordinarily that would be a case for the Washington police, except that the government had purchased the place a few days before; Tilliver was to move out the next day. Thus he was on government soil, and that put the case in our jurisdiction."

"I noticed the report was headed 'Suspect Unknown,' or something like that."

"Yes. We always do that until we have narrowed a case down to its essentials."

Jessup glanced at his watch.

"I've a few free minutes. Perhaps I could show you around."

"That would be a great privilege."

They walked together down the long hall. The inspector folded the sheaf of multigraphed reports.

"A queer affair, the Tilliver case. We'll all be glad to get it cleared up."

"I suppose you have to chase down every tiny lead."

"Everything. For instance, you perhaps know about the finding of a woman's shoe near the curbing and a pair of gloves, with blood on them, a half block away. Naturally we have to prove or disprove any connection between this evidence and the identity of the murderer."

"Then you know the killer?"

Jessup shook his head.

"Oh, I didn't say that. I said we're running down these clues. The investigation isn't completed. I'll let you watch an experiment or two in the laboratory if you're interested. I don't see how it could harm the case."

"I'd be delighted."

"First we'd better dip into the identification unit

21

if you want to see it again—the fingerprint section, you know." He opened a large pair of doors leading to a huge room, set with many metal filing cases. "Of course, you've been told how we classify the thousands of fingerprints received daily. Which reminds me—have you thought about introducing civil fingerprinting into your business? For identification, in case of illness, accident, amnesia, anything of that sort?"

"I've been thinking seriously about it," said Manton Kent.

"And, of course, your own fingerprints are on file here?"

"You mean in the file reserved for civil fingerprints? I'm sorry to say they're not."

"Well, of course, we never urge anyone to—"

"But I'd be delighted."

"Good. If you'll just step over this way." Then, at a table where stood a moist pad and a large card, clipped in a holder: "Now, your right hand first—just relax; I'll roll your fingers on this pad, then on the paper; it's really quite painless, unless, of course, a person has a criminal background—just relax again, Mr. Kent. Thank you. Now the other hand."

Manton Kent glanced at his fingers.

"I've always heard they'd be dirty from lampblack."

"No. This is a special pad and sensitized paper. It leaves no marks on the hands. Now, if you'll just fill out this card—your name, address, whom to notify in case of accident."

Manton Kent sat at a desk.

"It gives you a feeling of security, doesn't it?" he queried. Then, as he wrote: "I've been wondering why

22

you haven't been able to learn something by finger-prints about that murder case."

"You mean the Tilliver affair? Evidently the mur-derer wore gloves."

"Oh, of course."

Manton Kent finished the writing of his description and handed the completed card to the inspector. An agent happened to be passing. Jessup called him. "File this for Mr. Kent, please. Civil fingerprints."

The agent took the card and hurried away. Inspector Jessup turned to a dissertation on the fingerprint di-vision. At last: "Suppose now we step into the tech-nical division—the crime laboratory, as it is known." From a nearby corridor of filing cases, a machine began to whir. It caught the inspector's attention. "Before we leave the fingerprint section," he said hastily, "I want to show you how law enforcement has borrowed ideas from the business world."

"Yes?"

"By using an ordinary mechanical card sorter to catch crooks." He led the way to the machine, where a special agent and a fingerprint clerk were busily feeding it large stacks of cards, each punctured with many holes.

"An indexing machine," said Manton Kent. "We have a dozen of them in my organization."

"Of course. We merely adapted it to crooks. Instead of names or addresses, the prongs of that machine are set to fit into the holes in a card which designate one certain man's fingerprint classification. That big pile of cards the men are feeding it represents a search for a certain criminal. They are the records of every crook

23

who has a classification resembling that of the wanted man in any manner whatever. And if the crook we want is among them, this machine will find him." Manton Kent looked toward the side of the sorter, where two large slots appeared. One was rapidly filling with cards, representing rejections. The other was empty. The inspector said, "Let's stay and see if they find the fellow."

"Certainly."

A minute passed. The machine stopped, its piles of cards exhausted. The inspector turned away without waiting for the eye signal of the special agent to tell him that a search of the entire identification unit in the hope of finding some criminal reference to Manton Kent had been in vain.

"I suppose that machine is infallible," said Kent.

"If a record exists in the bureau," the inspector answered. "Unfortunately some of our enforcement bodies and prisons did not keep complete files prior to ten years ago. So in old cases we are always at a disadvantage."

"Unfortunate," answered Mr. Kent.

"Very. Shall we take a look at the crime laboratory?"

He led the way to another double door and held it wide for his guest. They entered an anteroom filled with exhibits of guns, an X-ray machine for looking into packages without unwrapping them, pictured histories of scientific crime detection in widely known cases.

"You've seen all this on the tours you've taken," said the inspector. "Let's go behind the scenes."

"Wonderful."

The inspector did not answer. He led the way into a big room that reeked with chemicals and stepped swiftly to a laboratory table where a sober-faced man in a white smock had apparently just completed a microscopic examination of a sheer silk stocking. Nearby, on the table, lay a woman's suede shoe.

"What experiment is this?" the inspector queried.

"The shoe is part of the Tilliver evidence," answered the scientist. "The stocking came from the room of Mrs. Bradford Bowen, in the Maytown Hotel."

Kent stepped closer.

"Oh, a suspect?"

The inspector smiled.

"Be patient, now. I'll show you how scientific detection works out. This, as you have guessed, is the woman's shoe that was found outside the Tilliver house after the murder. The next morning Mrs. Bowen reported to the hotel management that a shoe and a pair of gloves had been stolen from her room—that someone must have taken them while she was out."

"Easy enough," said Mr. Kent.

"Yes, of course. But we can't accept the palpable. So we conducted experiments to prove or disprove her story. You will notice that this stocking, which we obtained from her for experimental purposes, is of an extremely odd shade. We have determined that she never wears any other type. Therefore, microscopic examinations were made, both of the shoe and the stocking. The shoe revealed many tiny shreds of silk that match the fibers of this hose exactly. But the scientist could find no other fibers." He faced the besmocked laboratory man. "Is that correct, Moberton?"

"That is correct, sir—indicating that the shoe has not recently been on any other foot than that of this particular woman."

Manton Kent exhibited interest.

"Then you do have a suspect?"

"It begins to look that way. This experiment points suspicion either toward Mrs. Bowen or some person who may have stolen that shoe from her room in an attempt to divert suspicion toward her."

"That makes it a woman's deal all the way round, doesn't it?" asked Kent. "I see your deduction now. Two women are possibly in love with this Tilliver. One decides to kill him. So she steals a shoe and a pair of gloves from her rival and leaves them at the scene of the crime."

Jessup laughed and slapped Kent on the shoulder.

"The first thing you know, we'll be giving you an examination for the job of special agent. That's a very good deduction, except for the motive, which appears to have been blackmail—on Tilliver's part, not on that of the murderer."

Kent's eyes had widened.

"Oh, you've established that?"

"Is the evidence handy, Mr. Moberton?" asked the inspector. Then, following the scientist's glance, he moved toward a few pieces of charred paper under a glass cover. "This was found in the fireplace."

"But I don't see anything on it—merely some black ashes."

"Photography, under the ultraviolet ray, brought out the writing. Evidently Tilliver was in tight circumstances and knew somebody who was rich. Have you the photostatic copy of your experiment on this charred document, Mr. Moberton?"

Silently the scientist opened a drawer and brought out the photograph, while Kent stared in disbelief.

"It seems impossible!"

"Oh, we do lots of impossible things," Jessup said.

"You say that this letter was sent from Tilliver to someone else?"

"Yes. It has been determined to be Tilliver's writing." He referred to the photograph. "You will notice that this fragment of the letter says, 'I need a hundred thousand dollars and you have got it to give me. And unless you do give it to me, Old Pal, the reputation you have built up over all these years will not be worth five cents.' "

Manton Kent cleared his throat. "Is that all the writing you were able to recover?"

"Unfortunately that is all. Except for the beginning of the letter."

"You mean the name of the person to whom it was sent?"

"It was only 'Dear Pal.' "

"Unfortunate," exclaimed Manton Kent and gave his attention to the woman's shoe. The inspector eyed him closely; Kent's demeanor was that of enthusiastic interest and nothing more. Jessup turned.

"Suppose we see what experiments are being made with the gloves," he suggested and led the way with a pawlike hand on the suspect's shoulder. Again he sought to break through possible armor. "Perhaps I shouldn't dismiss that letter so lightly, because it really did aid us to some extent. It showed us the motive was a quarrel over blackmail. Tilliver had sent it to an old friend, apparently. That person evidently became wild with anger, rushed to Tilliver's house, stealing the shoe and gloves on the way. There was a fight or quarrel, at least a struggle—"

"I suppose you found chairs overturned and things like that?"

"No, nothing of the sort," the officer answered blandly and explained no further. "As I say, there was a struggle, and the murderer drew a pistol, killed Tilliver, remembered that the letter might be incriminating evidence, threw it in the fireplace, ran from the house, dropped the shoe at the curb, and threw away the gloves."

"And after that?" asked Kent.

Jessup shrugged.

"You know as much about that as I do," he answered with a grin. "Oh, here we are." He nodded to another besmocked man, who was busily dousing a pair of kid gloves in a laboratory tray filled with slightly discolored water. Jessup asked, in routine fashion, "This is an experiment with Tilliver evidence, Mr. Graves?"

The scientist, tall, freckled, sandy-haired, turned quietly.

"Yes, sir."

"Would you mind explaining it?"

"Not at all, sir. The object is to determine whether the murderer left his fingerprints on these gloves." He raised one from the tray with a rubber-shielded hand. "As you see, I have immersed the evidence in a solution of three percent nitrate of silver. I now place it

28

upon this large blotter and put it under this lamp—"

"Which is?"

"Ultraviolet rays, sir."

"And if there are fingerprints?"

"They will appear in a very few moments, of a brownish color, but perfectly detectable. Oh, by the way, an office messenger asked me to give you this memorandum."

The inspector took it, cupping it in his hand.

"Thank you," came briefly. Then, as the ultraviolet ray poured its weird light upon the saturated leather, Jessup glanced again at the memorandum.

12	25	W	100	17
4	aW	101	13

To Inspector Jessup these numbers became ridges and lines and whorls and deltas, assembling themselves into a mental picture of the fingerprints of this dapper, coldly calm man beside him. If once during this well-planned murder there had been a slip—if, for instance, there had been no protective covering for Manton Kent's fingers when these gloves were stolen—then the story would now be told.

Second after second the inspector waited. Twice he leaned forward as something brownish began to appear upon the white texture, only to draw back again.

"Only smudges," said the scientist, "from grease or a like substance."

"Yes, I see," answered Jessup. "And that was our big chance to nail him." Kent turned swiftly.

"Him?" he asked. "Then you don't think it was a woman?"

"Suppose we go over to the comparison micro-scope," replied the inspector. "I'll show you something interesting."

Again a besmocked man awaited them. Jessup asked for the murder gun. It was forthcoming—an automatic, blue-steeled, ugly, with the serial number filed off, to prevent tracing. The inspector held it out to Kent, who looked at it intently.

"This was found in a trash can some ten blocks from the murder scene," said Jessup. "You will note that it is a forty-five caliber. That is an extremely heavy gun for a woman to handle."

"Yes, I suppose so. But how do you know it is the murder gun?"

"If you'll come this way." He moved a few feet to what appeared to be a double-barreled microscope, fitted with a single eyepiece. "The comparison micro-scope," he said. "If you will remember, my theory is that there was a quarrel. Then Tilliver was shot. After the gun was found, a bullet was fired from it into a box of cotton, so that it might be recovered. Then the lethal bullet was extracted from the body of the mur-dered man.

"These two bullets were put on those prongs you see projecting beneath the lenses of the comparison microscope. Now, if you will look down through that eyepiece, you will see that the rifling of the gun barrel made distinctive marks on each of those bullets so that they exactly match." Kent bent forward. "You can see better if you'll take off your hat," added the inspector.

Manton Kent obeyed.

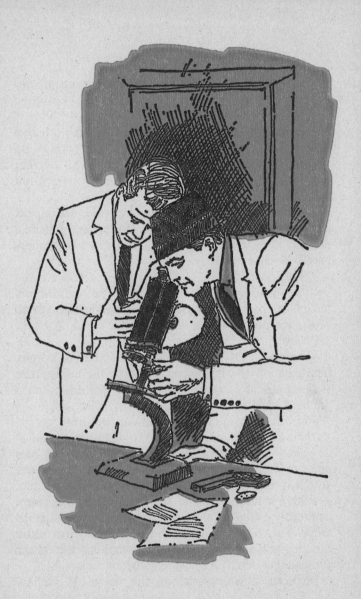

"I don't believe I quite get what you mean," he said, staring through the eyepiece.

"Perhaps the bullets are not in alignment. Just move that thumb set either forward or backward until the bullets come together——"

"Oh, this little gadget here?"

"Yes."

"Of course! I see the bullets begin to move, coming closer together——" Suddenly, with an ejaculation, he straightened, looking about him in surprised fashion. A hand went to the top of his head. "No bees around here?" he asked queerly.

"Bees? Why?"

"The queerest little jabbing pain hit me for an instant in the top of the head." He rubbed his scalp. "It's gone now."

"Neuralgia?"

"Probably, although I never had it before." Kent bent again to the microscope, moving the adjustment knobs until at last the two bullets seemed as one. "Remarkable!" he exclaimed.

Inspector Jessup touched him on an arm.

"Not half as remarkable as this final experiment," he said. "You will remember that I mentioned one piece of evidence as pointing to a struggle. Let's see how it is turning out in the hands of science."

With a hand on Manton Kent's arm, he led the way to another of the besmocked clan that peopled this big room. This time the scientist was a squat, pale man with a flat voice. He was surrounded by test tubes and chemical vials; a microscope stood before him.

Inspector Jessup went through his usual preliminary. "May I inquire, Mr. Caruth, what experiment you are conducting, and if it is the Tilliver case?"

"It is in the Tilliver case," came the toneless, precise voice as the scientist raised a cellophane container. "I have here two human hairs, each alike in size, color, thickness, texture, chemical analyses, and other characteristics both as to the fiber itself and to the follicles and adhering epithelia. One of these was found in the clutched hand of the murdered man, indicating that it had been torn from the head of the killer during a struggle. The other"—he looked up—"was, as you know, Inspector, just taken from the head of your guest as he bent over the comparison microscope."

Manton Kent gasped. He whirled, hands outstretched. Wildly his eyes sought the doorway—but two special agents stood there. Then Inspector Jessup's voice sounded, chilling in its cold courtesy:

"Will you please complete Mr. Kent's tour—by showing him to the detention quarters?"

THE BLAST OF THE BOOK

G. K. Chesterton

PROFESSOR OPENSHAW always lost his temper with a loud bang if anybody called him a spiritualist or a believer in spiritualism. This, however, did not exhaust his explosive elements, for he also lost his temper if anybody called him a disbeliever in spiritualism. It was his pride to have given his whole life to investigating psychic phenomena; it was also his pride never to have given a hint of whether he thought they were really psychic or merely phenomenal. He enjoyed nothing so much as to sit in a circle of devout spiritualists and give devastating descriptions of how he had exposed medium after medium and detected fraud after fraud: for indeed he was a man of much detective talent and insight, when once he had fixed his eye on an object, and he always fixed his eye on a medium as a highly suspicious object. There was a story of his having spotted the same spiritualistic mountebank under three different disguises: dressed as a woman, a white-bearded old man, and a Brahmin of a rich chocolate brown. These recitals made the true believers rather restless, as indeed they were intended to do; but they could hardly complain, for no spiritualist denies the existence of fraudulent mediums; only the professor's flowing narrative might well seem to indicate that all mediums were fraudulent.

But woe to the simpleminded and innocent materialist (and materialists as a race are rather innocent and simpleminded) who, presuming on this narrative tendency, should advance the thesis that ghosts were against the laws of nature, or that such things were only old superstitions, or that it was all tosh, or, alternatively, bunk. Him would the professor, suddenly reversing all his scientific batteries, sweep from the field with a cannonade of unquestionable cases and unexplained phenomena, of which the wretched rationalist had never heard in his life, giving all the dates and details, stating all the attempted and abandoned natural explanations, stating everything, indeed, except whether he, John Oliver Openshaw, did or did not believe in spirits, and that neither spiritualist nor materialist could ever boast of finding out.

Professor Openshaw, a lean figure with palleonine hair and hypnotic blue eyes, stood exchanging a few words with Father Brown, who was a friend of his, on the steps outside the hotel where both had been breakfasting that morning and sleeping the night before. The professor had come back rather late from one of his grand experiments in general exasperation and was still tingling with the fight that he always waged alone and against both sides.

"Oh, I don't mind you," he said, laughing. "You don't believe in it even if it's true. But all these people are perpetually asking me what I'm trying to prove. They don't seem to understand that I'm a man of science. A man of science isn't trying to prove anything. He's trying to find out what will prove itself."

"But he hasn't found out yet," said Father Brown.

"Well, I have some little notions of my own that are not quite so negative as most people think," answered the professor after an instant of frowning silence. "Anyhow, I've begun to fancy that if there is something to be found, they're looking for it along the wrong line. It's all too theatrical; it's showing off, all their shiny ectoplasm and trumpets and voices and the rest, all on the model of old melodramas and moldy historical novels about the family ghost. If they'd go to history instead of historical novels, I'm beginning to think they'd really find something. But not apparitions."

"After all," said Father Brown, "apparitions are only appearances. I suppose you'd say the family ghost is only keeping up appearances."

The professor's gaze, which had commonly a fine abstracted character, suddenly fixed and focused itself as it did on a dubious medium. It had rather the air of a man screwing a strong magnifying glass into his eye. Not that he thought the priest was in the least like a dubious medium, but he was startled into attention by his friend's thought following so closely on his own.

"Appearances!" he muttered. "Crikey, but it's odd you should say that just now. The more I learn, the more I fancy they lose by merely looking for appearances. Now, if they'd only begin to look a little into disappearances. . . ."

"Yes," said Father Brown, "after all, the real fairy legends weren't so very much about the appearance of famous fairies—calling up Titania or exhibiting Oberon by moonlight. But there were no end of legends about people *disappearing* because they were stolen by the fairies. Are you on the track of Kilmeny or Thomas the Rhymer?"

"I'm on the track of ordinary modern people you've read of in the newspapers," answered Openshaw. "You may well stare, but that's my game just now, and I've been on it for a long time. Frankly, I think a lot of psychic appearances could be explained away. It's the disappearances I can't explain, unless they're psychic. These people in the newspapers who vanish and are never found—if you knew the details as I do—and now only this morning I got confirmation, an extraordinary letter from an old missionary, quite a respectable old boy. He's coming to see me at my office this morning. Perhaps you'd lunch with me or something, and I'd tell the results—in confidence."

"Thanks. I will—unless," said Father Brown modestly, "the fairies have stolen me by then."

With that they parted and Openshaw walked round the corner to a small office he rented in the neighborhood, chiefly for the publication of a small periodical of psychical and psychological notes of the driest and most agnostic sort. He had only one clerk, who sat at a desk in the outer office, totting up figures and facts for the purposes of the printed report, and the professor paused to ask if Mr. Pringle had called. The clerk answered mechanically in the negative and went on mechanically adding up figures, and the professor turned toward the inner room that was his study. "Oh, by the way, Berridge," he added without turning round, "if Mr. Pringle comes, send him straight in to me. You needn't interrupt your work; I rather want those notes finished tonight if possible. You might leave them on my desk tomorrow if I am late."

And he went into his private office, still brooding on the problem which the name of Pringle had raised—or rather, perhaps, had ratified and confirmed in his mind. Even the most perfectly balanced of agnostics is partially human, and it is possible that the missionary's letter seemed to have greater weight as promising to support his private and still tentative hypothesis. He sat down in his large and comfortable chair, opposite the engraving of Montaigne, and read once more the short letter from the Reverend Luke Pringle, making the appointment for that morning. No man knew better than Professor Openshaw the marks of the letter of the crank—the crowded details, the spidery handwriting, the unnecessary length and repetition. There were none of these things in this case but a brief and businesslike typewritten statement that the writer had encountered some curious cases of disappearance, which seemed to fall within the province of the professor as a student of psychic problems. The professor was favorably impressed; nor had he any unfavorable impressions, in spite of a slight movement of surprise, when he looked up and saw that the Reverend Luke Pringle was already in the room.

"Your clerk told me I was to come straight in,"

said Mr. Pringle apologetically, but with a broad and rather agreeable grin. The grin was partly masked by masses of reddish-gray beard and whiskers—a perfect jungle of a beard, such as is sometimes grown by white men living in the jungles—but the eyes above the snub nose had nothing about them in the least wild or outlandish. Openshaw had instantly turned on them that concentrated spotlight or burning glass of skeptical scrutiny which he turned on many men to see if they were mountebanks or maniacs, and in this case he had a rather unusual sense of reassurance. The wild beard might have belonged to a crank, but the eyes completely contradicted the beard; they were full of that quite frank and friendly laughter which is never found in the faces of those who are serious frauds or serious lunatics. He would have expected a man with those eyes to be a Philistine, a jolly skeptic, a man who shouted out shallow but hearty contempt for ghosts and spirits; but, anyhow, no professional humbug could afford to look as frivolous as that. The man was buttoned up to the throat in a shabby old cape, and only his broad limp hat suggested the cleric. But missionaries from wild places do not always bother to dress like clerics.

"You probably think all this is another hoax, Professor," said Mr. Pringle with a sort of abstract enjoyment, "and I hope you will forgive my laughing at your very natural air of disapproval. All the same, I've got to tell my story to somebody who knows, because it's true. And, all joking apart, it's tragic as well as true. Well, to cut it short, I was a missionary in Nya-Nya, a station in West Africa, in the thick of

39

the forests, where almost the only other white man was the officer in command of the district, Captain Wales, and he and I grew rather thick. Not that he liked missions; he was, if I may say so, thick in many ways—one of those square-headed, square-shouldered men of action who hardly need to think, let alone believe. That's what makes it all the queerer. One day he came back to his tent in the forest, after a short leave, and said he had gone through a jolly rum experience and didn't know what to do about it. He was holding a rusty old book in a leather binding, and he put it down on a table beside his revolver and an old Arab sword he kept, probably as a curiosity. He said this book had belonged to a man on the boat he had just come off, and the man swore that nobody must open the book or look inside it, or else they would be carried off by the devil or disappear or something. Wales said this was all nonsense, of course, and they had a quarrel, and the upshot seems to have been that this man, taunted with cowardice or superstition, actually did look into the book, and instantly dropped it, walked to the side of the boat—"

"One moment," said the professor, who had made one or two notes. "Before you tell me anything else, did this man tell Wales where he had got the book or who it originally belonged to?"

"Yes," replied Pringle, now entirely grave. "It seems he said he was bringing it back to Dr. Hankey, the oriental traveler now in England, to whom it originally belonged, and who had warned him of its strange properties. Well, Hankey is an able man and a rather crabbed and sneering sort of man, which makes it queerer still. But the point of Wales's story is much simpler. It is that the man who had looked into the book walked straight over the side of the ship and was never seen again."

"Do you believe it yourself?" asked Openshaw after a pause.

"Well, I do," replied Pringle. "I believe it for two reasons. First, that Wales was an entirely unimaginative man, and he added one touch that only an imaginative man could have added. He said that the man walked straight over the side on a still and calm day, but there was no splash."

The professor looked at his notes for some seconds in silence and then said, "And your other reason for believing it?"

"My other reason," answered the Reverend Luke Pringle, "is what I saw myself."

There was another silence until he continued in the same matter-of-fact way. Whatever he had, he had nothing of the eagerness with which the crank, or even the believer, tries to convince others.

"I told you that Wales put down the book on the table beside the sword. There was only one entrance to the tent, and it happened that I was standing in it, looking out into the forest, with my back to my companion. He was standing by the table grumbling and growling about the whole business, saying it was tomfoolery in the twentieth century to be frightened of opening a book, asking why the devil he shouldn't open it himself. Then some instinct stirred in me and I said that he had better not do that, it had better be returned to Dr. Hankey. 'What harm could it do?' he said restlessly. 'What harm did it do?' I answered obstinately. 'What happened to your friend on the boat?' He didn't answer; indeed, I didn't know what he could answer, but I pressed my logical advantage in mere vanity. 'If it comes to that,' I said, 'what is your version of what really happened on the boat?' Still he didn't answer, and I looked round and saw that he wasn't there.

"The tent was empty. The book was lying on the table, open, but on its face, as if he had turned it downward. But the sword was lying on the ground near the other side of the tent, and the canvas of the tent showed a great slash, as if somebody had hacked his way out with the sword. The gash in the tent gaped at me but showed only the dark glimmer of the forest outside. And when I went across and looked through the rent I could not be certain whether the tangle of the tall plants and the undergrowth had been bent or broken, at least not farther than a few feet. I have never seen or heard of Captain Wales from that day.

"I wrapped the book up in brown paper, taking good care not to look at it, and I brought it back to England, intending at first to return it to Dr. Hankey. Then I saw some notes in your paper suggesting a hypothesis about such things, and I decided to stop on the way and put the matter before you, as you have a name for being balanced and having an open mind."

Professor Openshaw laid down his pen and looked steadily at the man on the other side of the table, concentrating in that single stare all his long experience of many entirely different types of humbug, and even some eccentric and extraordinary types of honest men. In the ordinary way, he would have begun with the healthy hypothesis that the story was a pack of lies. On the whole, he did incline to assume that it was a pack of lies. And yet he could not fit the man into his story, if it were only that he could not see that sort of liar telling that sort of lie. The man was not trying to look honest on the surface, as most quacks and impostors do. Somehow it seemed all the other way, as if the man *was* honest, in spite of something else that was merely on the surface. He thought of a good man with one innocent delusion, but again the symptoms were not the same; there was even a sort of virile indifference, as if the man did not care much about his delusion, if it was a delusion.

"Mr. Pringle," he said sharply, like a barrister making a witness jump, "where is this book of yours now?"

The grin reappeared on the bearded face, which had grown grave during the recital.

"I left it outside," said Mr. Pringle. "I mean in the outer office. It was a risk, perhaps, but the less risk of the two."

"What do you mean?" demanded the professor. "Why didn't you bring it straight in here?"

"Because," answered the missionary, "I knew that as soon as you saw it, you'd open it—before you had heard the story. I thought it possible you might think twice about opening it—after you'd heard the story."

Then after a silence he added, "There was nobody out there but your clerk, and he looked a stolid steady-going specimen, immersed in business calculations."

43

Openshaw laughed unaffectedly. "Oh, Babbage," he cried. "Your magic tomes are safe enough with him, I assure you. His name's Berridge—but I often call him Babbage, because he's so exactly like a calculating machine. No human being, if you can call him a human being, would be less likely to open other people's brown-paper parcels. Well, we may as well go and bring it in now, though I assure you I will consider seriously the course to be taken with it. Indeed, I tell you frankly," and he stared at the man again, "that I'm not quite sure whether we ought to open it here and now or send it to this Dr. Hankey."

The two had passed together out of the inner into the outer office, and even as they did so Mr. Pringle gave a cry and ran forward toward the clerk's desk. For the clerk's desk was there, but not the clerk. On the clerk's desk lay a faded old leather book, torn out of its brown-paper wrappings and lying closed, but as if it had just been opened. The clerk's desk stood against the wide window that looked out into the street, and the window was shattered with a huge ragged hole in the glass, as if a human body had been shot through it into the world without. There was no other trace of Mr. Berridge.

Both the two men left in the office stood as still as statues, and then it was the professor who slowly came to life. He looked even more judicial than he had ever looked in his life as he slowly turned and held out his hand to the missionary.

"Mr. Pringle," he said, "I beg your pardon. I beg your pardon only for thoughts that I have had, and half-thoughts at that. But nobody could call himself

a scientific man and not face a fact like this."

"I suppose," said Pringle doubtfully, "that we ought to make some inquiries. Can you ring up his house and find out if he has gone home?"

"I don't know that he's on the telephone," answered Openshaw rather absently. "He lives somewhere up Hampstead way, I think. But I suppose somebody will inquire here if his friends or family miss him."

"Could we furnish a description," asked the other, "if the police want it?"

"The police!" said the professor, starting from his reverie. "A description. . . . Well, he looked awfully like everybody else, I'm afraid, except for goggles. One of those clean-shaven chaps. But the police. . . . Look here, what *are* we to do about this business?"

"I know what I ought to do," said the Reverend Mr. Pringle firmly. "I am going to take this book straight to the only original Dr. Hankey and ask him what the devil it's all about. He lives not very far from here, and I'll come straight back and tell you what he says."

"Oh, very well," said the professor at last as he sat down rather wearily, perhaps relieved for the moment to be rid of the responsibility. But long after the brisk and ringing footsteps of the little missionary had died away down the street the professor sat in the same posture, staring into vacancy like a man in a trance.

He was still in the same seat and almost in the same attitude when the same brisk footsteps were heard on the pavement without and the missionary entered, this time, as a glance assured him, with empty hands.

"Dr. Hankey," said Pringle gravely, "wants to keep

the book for an hour and consider the point. Then he asks us both to call, and he will give us his decision. He specially desired, Professor, that you should accompany me on the second visit."

Openshaw continued to stare in silence. Then he said suddenly, "Who the devil is Dr. Hankey?"

"You sound rather as if you meant he was the devil," said Pringle, smiling, "and I fancy some people have thought so. He had quite a reputation in your own line, but he gained it mostly in India, studying local magic and so on, so perhaps he's not so well known here. He is a yellow, skinny little devil with a lame leg and a doubtful temper, but he seems to have set up in an ordinary respectable practice in these parts, and I don't know anything definitely wrong about him—unless it's wrong to be the only person who can possibly know anything about all this crazy affair."

Professor Openshaw rose heavily and went to the telephone; he rang up Father Brown, changing the luncheon engagement to a dinner, that he might hold himself free for the expedition to the house of the Anglo-Indian doctor. After that he sat down again, lit a cigar, and sank once more in his own unfathomable thoughts.

Father Brown went round to the restaurant appointed for dinner and kicked his heels for some time in a vestibule full of mirrors and palms in pots. He had been informed of Openshaw's afternoon engagement and, as the evening closed in dark and stormy round the glass and the green plants, guessed that it had

47

produced something unexpected and unduly prolonged. He even wondered for a moment whether the professor would turn up at all, but when the professor eventually did, it was clear that his own more general guesses had been justified. For it was a very wild-eyed and even wild-haired professor who eventually drove back with Mr. Pringle from the expedition to the north of London, where suburbs are still fringed with healthy wastes and scraps of common, looking more somber under the rather thunderous sunset. Nevertheless, they had apparently found the house, standing a little apart though within hail of other houses; they had verified the brass plate duly engraved "J. D. Hankey, M.D., M.R.C.S." Only they did not find J. D. Hankey, M.D., M.R.C.S. They found only what a nightmare whisper had already subconsciously prepared them to find: a commonplace parlor with the accursed volume lying on the table, as if it had just been read, and beyond, a back door burst open and a faint trail of footsteps that ran a little way up so steep a garden path that it seemed that no lame man could have run up so lightly. But it was a lame man who had run; for those few steps there was the misshapen, unequal mark of some sort of surgical boot, then two marks of that boot alone (as if the creature had hopped), and then nothing. There was nothing further to be learned from Dr. J. D. Hankey, except that he had made his decision. He had read the oracle and received the doom.

When the two came into the entrance under the palms, Pringle put the book down suddenly on a small table, as if it burned his fingers. The priest glanced at it curiously; there was only some rude lettering on the front with a couplet:

> They that looked into this book,
> Them the Flying Terror took;

and underneath, as he afterward discovered, similar warnings in Greek, Latin, and French. The other two had turned away with a natural impulsion toward drinks, after their exhaustion and bewilderment, and Openshaw had called to the waiter, who brought cocktails on a tray.

"You will dine with us, I hope," said the professor to the missionary, but Mr. Pringle amiably shook his head.

"If you'll forgive me," he said, "I'm going off to wrestle with this book and this business by myself somewhere. I suppose I couldn't use your office for an hour or so?"

"I suppose—I'm afraid it's locked," said Openshaw in some surprise.

"You forget, there's a hole in the window." The Reverend Luke Pringle gave the very broadest of all his grins and vanished into the darkness without.

"A rather odd fellow, that, after all," said the professor, frowning.

He was rather surprised to find Father Brown talking to the waiter who had brought the cocktails, apparently about the waiter's most private affairs, for there was some mention of a baby who was now out of danger. He commented on the fact with some surprise, wondering how the priest came to know the man, but the former only said, "Oh, I dine here every two or three months, and I've talked to him now and then."

The professor, who himself dined there about five times a week, was conscious that he had never thought of talking to the man, but his thoughts were interrupted by a strident ringing and a summons to the telephone. The voice on the telephone said it was Pringle. It was rather a muffled voice, but it might well be muffled in all those bushes of beard and whisker. Its message was enough to establish identity.

"Professor," said the voice, "I can't stand it any longer. I'm going to look for myself. I'm speaking from your office, and the book is in front of me. If anything happens to me, this is to say good-bye. No— it's no good trying to stop me. You wouldn't be in time, anyhow. I'm opening the book now. I . . . ."

Openshaw thought he heard something like a sort of thrilling or shivering yet almost soundless crash; then he shouted the name of Pringle again and again, but he heard no more. He hung up the receiver and, restored to a superb academic calm, rather like the calm of despair, went back and quietly took his seat at the dinner table. Then, as coolly as if he were describing the failure of some small silly trick at a séance, he told the priest every detail of this monstrous mystery.

"Five men have now vanished in this impossible way," he said. "Every one is extraordinary, and yet the one case I simply can't get over is my clerk, Berridge. It's just because he was the quietest creature that he's the queerest case."

"Yes," replied Father Brown, "it was a queer thing

for Berridge to do, anyway. He was awfully conscientious. He was always so jolly careful to keep all the office business separate from any fun of his own. Why, hardly anybody knew he was quite a humorist at home and—"

"Berridge!" cried the professor. "What on earth are you talking about? Did you know him?"

"Oh, no," said Father Brown carelessly, "only as you say I know the waiter. I've often had to wait in your office till you turned up, and of course I passed the time of day with poor Berridge. He was rather a card. I remember he once said he would like to collect valueless things, as collectors did the silly things they thought valuable. You know the old story about the woman who collected valueless things."

"I'm not sure I know what you're talking about," said Openshaw. "But even if my clerk was eccentric (and I never knew a man I should have thought less so), it wouldn't explain what happened to him, and it certainly wouldn't explain the others."

"What others?" asked the priest.

The professor stared at him and spoke distinctly, as if to a child.

"My dear Father Brown, five men have disappeared."

"My dear Professor Openshaw, no men have disappeared."

Father Brown gazed back at his host with equal steadiness and spoke with equal distinctness. Nevertheless, the professor required the words repeated, and they were repeated as distinctly.

"I say that no men have disappeared."

51

After a moment's silence, he added, "I suppose the hardest thing is to convince anybody that zero plus zero plus zero equals zero. Men believe the oddest things if they are in a series; that is why Macbeth believed the three words of the three witches, though the first was something he knew himself, and the last something he could only bring about himself. But in your case the middle term is the weakest of all."

"What do you mean?"

"You saw nobody vanish. You did not see the man vanish from the boat. You did not see the man vanish from the tent. All that rests on the word of Mr. Pringle, which I will not discuss just now. But you'll admit this: You would never have taken his word yourself *unless* you had seen it confirmed by your clerk's disappearance, just as Macbeth would never have believed he would be king if he had not been confirmed in believing he would be Cawdor."

"That may be true," said the professor, nodding slowly. "But *when* it was confirmed, I knew it was the truth. You say I saw nothing myself. But I did; I saw my own clerk disappear. Berridge did disappear."

"Berridge did not disappear," said Father Brown. "On the contrary."

"What the devil do you mean by 'on the contrary'?"

"I mean," said Father Brown, "that he never disappeared. He appeared."

Openshaw stared across at his friend, but the eyes had already altered in his head, as they did when they concentrated on a new presentation of a problem.

The priest went on: "He appeared in your study, disguised in a bushy red beard and buttoned up in a clumsy cape, and announced himself as the Reverend Luke Pringle. And you had never noticed your own clerk enough to know him again, when he was in so rough-and-ready a disguise."

"But surely . . ." began the professor.

"Could you describe him for the police?" asked Father Brown. "Not you. You probably knew he was clean-shaven and wore tinted glasses, and merely taking off those glasses was a better disguise than putting on anything else. You had never seen his eyes any more than his soul—jolly laughing eyes. He had planted his absurd book and all the properties; then he calmly smashed the window, put on the beard and cape, and walked into your study, knowing that you had never looked at him in your life."

"But why should he play me such an insane trick?" demanded Openshaw.

"Why, *because* you had never looked at him in your life," said Father Brown, and his hand slightly curled and clinched, as if he might have struck the table, if he had been given to gesture. "You called him the calculating machine because that was all you ever used him for. You never found out even what a stranger strolling into your office could find out in five minutes' chat: that he was a character, that he was full of antics, that he had all sorts of views on you and your theories and your reputation for 'spotting' people. Can't you understand his itching to prove that you couldn't spot your own clerk? He has nonsense notions of all sorts. About collecting useless things, for instance. Don't you know the story of the woman who bought the two most useless things, an old doctor's brass plate and a wooden leg? With those your ingenious clerk created the character of the remarkable Dr. Hankey as easily as the visionary Captain Wales. Planting them in his own house—"

"Do you mean that place we visited beyond Hampstead was Berridge's own house?" asked Openshaw.

"Did *you* know his house—or even his address?" retorted the priest. "Look here, don't think I'm speaking disrespectfully of you or your work. You are a great servant of truth and you know I could never be disrespectful to that. You've seen through a lot of liars, when you put your mind to it. But don't *only* look at liars. Do, just occasionally, look at honest men —like the waiter."

"Where is Berridge now?" asked the professor after a long silence.

"I haven't the least doubt," said Father Brown, "that he is back in your office. In fact, he came back into your office at the exact moment when the Reverend Luke Pringle read the volume and faded into the void."

There was another long silence and then Professor Openshaw laughed—with the laugh of a great man who is great enough to look small. Then he said abruptly: "I suppose I do deserve it, for not noticing the nearest helpers I have. But you must admit the accumulation of incidents was rather formidable. Did you *never* feel just a momentary awe of the awful volume?"

"Oh, that," said Father Brown. "I opened it as soon as I saw it lying there. It's all blank pages. You see, I am not superstitious."

THE MISSING UNDERGRADUATE

Henry Wade

As THE EXPRESS neared Oxford and began to slow down, Detective-Inspector John Poole gazed eagerly out of the right-hand windows in search of the familiar landmarks. He had not been back to Oxford since he "came down" in 1921; a year later he had joined the metropolitan police, and hard work, combined with settled policy, had cut him off from nearly all his old associations.

Now he was coming down on duty. A message had reached Scotland Yard that morning asking for a detective to be sent down to investigate the disappearance of an undergraduate of St. Peter's College, and Superintendent Wylde, aware of Poole's early training, had thought that his local knowledge might prove useful.

Poole knew nothing more of the case than he had seen in the papers, which had treated as a young man's escapade the disappearance of Gerald Catling four days previously, but now apparently the college authorities were beginning to take an alarmist view of the occurrence and, presumably doubting the capacity of the city police, had applied for help from headquarters.

Ah, there they were, the "dreaming spires"—Magdalen's tower on the right—its modest counterpart, Merton, farther to the left—St. Mary's—in the foreground the old castle from which Queen Matilda had fled across the snow in 1141—behind it "Old Tom," the magnificent gate tower of Christ Church, a handsome king lording it among his court of lovely princesses.

The train slowed down abruptly. Poole swung his small suitcase from the rack and within five minutes was presenting himself to the porter of St. Peter's and asking for the warden. The dignified official looked suspiciously at his card, and with obvious reluctance, after directing him to place his bag out of the way of the young gentlemen's bicycles, led the way into Bacchus Quad.

"The warden is indisposed," he threw over his shoulder. "Mr. Luddingham will see you."

Poole gasped. The warden of St. Peter's he had known vaguely by sight, and in his turn had been unknown. But Luddingham, the dean, had been his own lecturer in constitutional law. With the Oxford tradition of long memory, there was not the faintest chance of the dean failing to recognize him. With mingled feelings of shyness and pride, Poole followed his guide up the center staircase of the quad to a doorway on the first floor, over which was written in white letters on a small black tablet: MR. LUDDINGHAM. Leaving the detective on the landing, the porter went in with his card, returning at once with an invitation to enter.

The dean was standing with his back to a large open fireplace in which a huge log of fir spluttered blue flames up the vast chimney. Not a sign of surprise or recognition was visible upon his pale, clean-shaven face. He waved to a chair.

"Good morning, Inspector," he said. "Good of you to come so quickly. Have they told you anything about this business?"

"Nothing, sir. I've seen the papers—that's all."

"And that's all wrong, needless to say. I'll give you the facts as I know them; then you can ask questions. Smoke if you want to."

His hands clasped behind his back, his gray eyes fixed upon the angle of ceiling and wall opposite him, and raising himself from time to time onto his toes, the dean gave forth his information in exactly the same dry, succinct manner as he employed in the delivery of a lecture upon the work of Bagehot or Stubbs.

"Gerald Trefusis Catling came up to this college from Harrow in the Michaelmas term of last year, 1928. He is the only son of Sir John Trefusis Catling, of Gardham Manor, Wakestone, Yorkshire, and his age is nineteen years and ten months. He has passed Moderations and is now reading for his Final School.

"On Friday last he did not return to college before twelve; his absence was reported to me in the ordinary course by the head porter. He did not attend roll call the following morning, and after making some inquiries from his tutor and some of his friends, I telephoned to his father at the House of Commons—where he represents the Wakestone division in the Conservative interest. His father replied that he knew nothing of his son's movements and that in all probability his absence was some form of practical joke. I should say that the boy has a leaning toward that form of humor and has on more than one occasion in his year and a half of residence been at issue with both the college and university authorities in consequence thereof.

"When Saturday night passed and he still did not return, I asked Sir John to come down here. He did so and was still inclined to treat the matter lightly, refusing any suggestion of reference to the police. On Monday evening, however, I received a letter from Lady Catling, written from Wakestone, saying that she was seriously alarmed, that, though her son was certainly fond of practical jokes, she was quite sure that he would not go to the length of frightening her in the way that his prolonged and unexplained absence from college must inevitably do, and asking me to take more active steps to find him.

"I again telephoned to Sir John late last night, asking for his concurrence to my calling in the help of the city police; he replied that if the thing was to be done at all, it had better be done thoroughly, and asked me to communicate direct with Scotland Yard. He explained that he had to go over to France by the early boat train, and would not, therefore, be able to take any action in the matter himself. He gave me full authority to act as I thought fit and an address in Paris to which to write. I telephoned to Scotland Yard first thing this morning, with the result that you know."

Poole had jotted down some notes as Mr. Luddingham's lecture proceeded; after finishing them, he thought for a moment and then asked, "Was Mr. Catling known to be in any trouble, serious or slight?"

The dean shook his head.

"The last word I should apply to him—he didn't know the meaning of it, I should say."

"Not in debt?"

"Not more than fifty percent of the members of this college are—a few tailors' and photographers' bills, perhaps!"

"No enemies?"

"Not serious. Of course, he was a nuisance at times, with his practical jokes." Poole gathered the impression that the missing undergraduate had been rather a thorn in the flesh of his dean.

"When was he last seen?"

Before Mr. Luddingham could answer, there was a knock at the door, and in response to his reply a tall, gaunt man of about sixty, with drooping, tawny moustache and wearing a gown and mortarboard, came in.

"Oh, Luddingham," he said, "I just called in on my way back from my lecture to ask if you'd got any news of Catling."

"None, I'm afraid, Cayzer," replied the dean. "No doubt he'll be back today, though." He did not attempt

59

to introduce his two visitors to one another. The tall don looked nervously from one to the other, fidgeting with his gown.

"So strange," he said, "so sad—a charming, high-spirited boy!" He paused, sighed heavily, and, turning abruptly, strode out of the room.

Poole looked inquiringly at the dean.

"Professor Cayzer," said the latter, evidently loath to bring in any matter that he considered unessential. "Chair of Egyptology. A member of this college. You asked when Catling was last seen. His scout took lunch to his rooms at the usual time—one thirty. He was there then, and nobody seems to have seen him after that. He was not seen to leave college, but it is perfectly possible for him to have done so unnoticed, if the porter was engaged—telephoning or making an entry in his book."

"Had he a car?"

"Yes, at the City Motor Company's garage in Gloucester Street, but he didn't use it that day—or subsequently."

"Nothing was seen of him at the station?"

"I haven't inquired; that is more in the line of the police."

After obtaining from Mr. Luddingham an approximate estimate of Catling's debts and a few further details about his habits and characteristics, Poole rose to his feet.

"If I may have a recent photograph, sir, and see one or two of Mr. Catling's friends?"

The dean thought for a minute.

"Yes," he said. "I'll send for Monash—he'll be back

from his logic lecture by now. He'll put you on to others and get a photograph. You'd better have my third room—I don't want more commotion about this business than is absolutely necessary. Perhaps you would ask anyone you interview to keep quiet about it—though I don't suppose they will!"

Ten minutes later Poole, in the tiny "thirder" which the dean had fitted up as a supernumerary study, was interviewing Crispin Monash, young Catling's contemporary and particular friend. Monash was a rowing man—a robust, unimaginative person who was able to give Poole just the bare, unadorned facts that he required.

From his account it appeared that Catling was not quite the featherbrained young man that Poole had pictured from the dean's description. He certainly was fond of ragging people and rather fancied himself as an impersonator—he was already a prominent member of the O.U.D.S.—but he was also quite serious in his determination to take a good degree and to follow in his father's footsteps as an administrator. Monash thought that his friend had been rather worried about his financial affairs lately, but not to the extent of doing anything desperate about them.

"He didn't give you any indication of something unusual being up on Friday?" asked the detective.

"Nothing. Don't think I saw him, except at 'Rollers.' We didn't as a rule see much of each other before tea —taking different schools, and in the afternoon I row, and he doesn't do anything serious—squash occasionally. I haven't the faintest idea what he's up to."

"Tell me quite frankly, sir: Do you think this is

either a practical joke or suicide?"

Monash gave the question careful consideration.

"No, I don't," he said. "I don't believe he'd carry a joke so far. As to suicide, he's the last chap—well, not the last, perhaps, but he's not that sort. I don't know what to think!"

"What about friends—is he liked?"

"Oh, yes. Popular sort of chap. Willan—running blue—Collerack and Vace are his particular friends, I should say—and myself. They'll tell you much what I have."

"Enemies?"

"Don't think so. Of course, some men didn't care for him—he used to rise the saps rather—but nothing serious."

"And the dons?"

"There again, the younger ones liked him—he amused them—but the older ones—the dean and so on—were rather bored by him—thought he went a bit too far, I suppose."

"One of the older ones seemed to have liked him," said Poole. "Professor Cayzer was inquiring about him just now, when I was with the dean—he seemed upset about him."

"Old Cat-Gut?" Monash looked surprised. "I should have thought Gerry bored him more than any of 'em! The old chap's got a private museum in his rooms, and Gerry used to rag him about it—pretend he was fearfully keen on some dry subject. Cayzer always fell for it—he's a bit potty, I think—and then Gerry gradually pulled his leg harder and harder, till at last the old chap couldn't help tumbling to it. I should have thought he rather barred him."

"Apparently not, sir. One does find that; old people rather like being teased by young ones, if it's not done maliciously. Now I must see some of his other friends. Can you get hold of them for me?"

For the next hour Poole listened to the view of Messrs. Willan, Collerack, and Vace, but apart from a statement by the first that he believed Gerry Catling had gone on a tour with a company that had been at the theater last week, and with two of whose members he had struck up an enthusiastic friendship, nothing significant emerged. It was evidently time to substitute looking for listening. In response to the detective's request, Mr. Luddingham sent for Gerald Catling's scout, Pelfett, and instructed him to show Inspector Poole Mr. Catling's rooms and give him any information he required.

The two minutes' walk from the dean's rooms to those of Mr. Catling, in New Quad, were sufficient to reveal Pelfett's opinion of his charge. The elderly scout exactly represented the type that Poole had sketched to Monash—he snarled about the young gentleman's habit of teasing him, but evidently had a genuine fondness for him. He thought it quite obvious that Mr. Catling had absented himself with the sole object of irritating the dean—had he not already succeeded by bringing a Scotland Yard 'tec into the sacred precincts of St. Peter's? The degradation implied by this remark tickled Poole immensely.

Pelfett would clearly have liked to dispose of the intruder after a cursory glance at Mr. Catling's rooms, but Poole firmly reversed the process, and, having closed the heavy outer door to insure freedom from interruption, set about a systematic survey of the missing man's environment—for here, he felt, must he look for the clue to the mystery.

It was in the bedroom, Poole thought, that young Catling's identity most clearly revealed itself. On the mantelpiece was a large photograph of a charming middle-aged lady, obviously "Mother"; on either side of it a vase of daffodils, now dead—Poole felt an unreasoning desire to kick the idle scout. On the chest of drawers was a small snapshot of a man in hunting kit—probably "Father." Poole felt from this, and from what he had heard from the dean, that there was no close bond of affection between father and son. Above the boy's bed was a reproduction of "Lux Mundi," and on a chair beside it, a well-worn Bible and a copy of Stevenson's *Virginibus Puerisque*.

A locked dispatch box in a drawer of the writing table was the first item to attract Poole's interest. It was a simple affair and soon yielded to the insinuations of a skeleton key. Inside was a bundle of letters— a quick glance revealed them as entirely harmless love letters of the calf variety—a checkbook, a passbook, and a file of receipts and bills. In a separate pocket was a single letter, in a strong, angular hand, which dealt fluently and unsympathetically with the subject of debt; it was dated a month back and was signed "Your affect. father." This might be important.

A drawer of the bedroom chest of drawers revealed a box of makeup, crepe hair, greasepaint, coconut butter, spirit gum, and soiled towels, all complete— the tools of Mr. Catling's hobby. The clothes were good in quality but modest in quantity, and they were well cared for. On the dressing table, among brushes and stud boxes, lay a small heap of papers—a letter from "Your ever loving mother," a theater program, one sheet of an essay, and a torn fragment of type-written notepaper.

The scrap was so small that Poole nearly over-looked it, but a second glance showed that it might be important. It appeared to be part of a dunning letter and ran as follows:

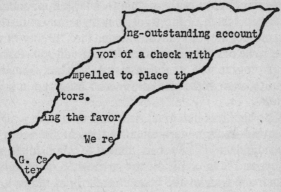

ng-outstanding account

vor of a check with

mpelled to place th

tors.

ing the favor

We re

G. Ca
ter

A straightforward demand, and probably not a very deadly one, but to an inexperienced youth who had lately been in trouble with his father on the subject of debt, it might represent a very real calamity.

In any case, it should not be too difficult to trace it to its source, and, armed with this and a list of Mr. Catling's tradesmen, culled from the files of receipts and bills, the detective made his way out of college.

His first action was to report to the headquarters of the city police and endeavor to make his peace with them and enlist their help. Fortunately the superintendent in charge was a broad-minded man, and Poole's line of conciliation and respect soon caused him to forget the slight he and his force had suffered at the hands of the college authorities—Poole explained that it was really Sir John Catling's doing.

The superintendent accepted the photograph of Gerald Catling which Monash had given to Poole and promised to have discreet inquiries made at the railway stations. He could not identify the authorship of the dunning letter but was able to advise the Scotland Yard man which of the tradesmen figuring on his list was most likely to have resorted to it. Curiously enough, he did not point to the large creditors—tailors and photographers, as the dean had shrewdly guessed —but to some of the smaller fry who might be in need of cash.

"The big firms like to let their accounts run on right to the end of an undergraduate's time here," said the superintendent. "They can afford to wait for their money, and long credit means large interest—if nothing more. I wonder the college authorities allow it, I must say."

Poole's round of visits to Catling's tradesmen, however—even though it was extended to include the greatest and the least of them—produced no result. A bright idea took him to a leading stationer who, after a close examination of the scrap of paper, opined that it did not emanate from any firm in Oxford. It was superfine paper, distinctly costly, and not at all such as was likely to be wasted upon unobservant undergraduates—pearls before swine, in fact. It was much more likely to belong to some very high-class and select London firm—something a cut above tailors, at that.

This was more interesting, and as it was really the only clue he had to work on, Poole decided to return to London and follow it up at once. Having ascertained from the dean that a thorough search of the college premises and cross-examination of the gate porters had already been made, without result, he caught the 5:00 P.M. train back to town and before seven was closeted with the stationery expert at Scotland Yard.

Detective-Inspector Bodley, having always evinced a marked capacity in that direction, was now employed on little but the examination and classification of stationery, printing, and ink. His work was of extraordinary value to his colleagues, as his almost uncanny powers enabled him to reduce their fields of search in this subject to very conscribed limits. One glance at the scrap of paper enabled him to tell Poole what firm —fortunately a Thames-side one—had made it.

It was too late to do any more that evening except to have dinner and, over a cup of coffee and a pipe, think out the problem upon which, as yet, so little light had been shed. The detective felt instinctively opposed to the idea of suicide—a high-spirited boy of the type of Gerald Catling surely could not take life so seriously as to quail before a simple money trouble. Practical joke was more possible, but plain disappearance, such as this, was so senseless—and so cruel. Accident seemed much more probable, but it was difficult to believe that such a thing could remain undiscovered in a crowded hive of busy life like Oxford.

Foul play was surely out of the question in such an environment.

Ten o'clock on the following morning found Poole in the office of the Blackfriars Paper Manufacturing Company. The manager recognized the specimen shown to him as being one of the highest grade papers produced by his firm—Imperial Bond. Only three stationers in London stocked it—one in the city, one in Holborn, and one in Kingsway. To each in turn went Poole, gathering a list of firms supplied, which, select though it might be, was still long enough to make him dislike the prospect of interviewing them all. Poole decided first of all to see whether Inspector Bodley could not in some way whittle down the list. He had identified the paper; perhaps he could do the same for the typewriter that had performed on it.

This was exactly what Inspector Bodley, on inquiry, could do. The typewriter used was a No. 3 Chanticleer —an expensive model which was not too common. This further known factor reduced the problem to workable proportions; it was an easy matter for three men at Scotland Yard, on three separate telephone lines, to run through the list of firms and inquire whether a No. 3 Chanticleer typewriter was used by them. The result exceeded Poole's highest hopes— only two firms used both Imperial Bond paper and a No. 3 Chanticleer typewriter: the Archaeological Supply Association and the Connoisseur Book Company. Both were in the neighborhood of Kingsway, and Poole, taking a taxi, drove to the nearest.

The manager of the Archaeological Supply Association received Poole in his office with dignified restraint. The atmosphere of the place—somber, dark, redolent somehow of the dead past—had impressed itself upon the detective's spirits as he made his way through the cases of fossils, scarabs, mummified cats, and other treasures so dear to the expert, so dispiriting to the layman. He unconsciously lowered his voice as he spoke.

"Can you tell me whether the letter of which this scrap is a part came from your office, sir?"

The manager scrutinized it with judicial lack of interest.

"If it did, it is clearly a confidential matter. May I ask why you are inquiring about it?"

"I am investigating the disappearance of an undergraduate—at Oxford. I have reason to believe that this particular letter to him may be connected with his disappearance."

"To an undergraduate?" The manager allowed the shadow of a smile to cross his face. "I can give you my assurance that this letter is not in any way connected with an undergraduate. It does, as you have surmised, emanate from this office—though how you discovered that I fail to understand—but—it clearly has reached your hand in error."

"But it's got his name on it! Look—'G. Ca . . .'— obviously the beginning of 'G. Catling'—Gerald Catling—'St. Peter's College,' too—his address."

The manager looked keenly at Poole.

"I see I shall have to divulge a confidential matter," he said. "It will, of course, go no further?"

"Not unless it is necessary in the interests of justice."

"Then I will tell you. This letter was addressed to

Professor Grantham Cayzer, holder of the Assington Chair of Egyptology at Oxford University. He also resides, by what appears to be an astonishing coincidence, at St. Peter's College."

Poole was flabbergasted. "Old Cat-Gut"—as Monash had disrespectfully called him—being dunned for a bill like any young rake! The manager evidently read what was passing in his mind and hastened to justify his firm's action.

"The course we have taken in the matter has been most distasteful to us," he said, "but when I tell you that we have received no payment over five years for an account that has risen into four figures, I think you will see that there had to be some limit—this letter, of course, is the last of a series. When I add that there is talk of the professor—but that is going beyond my brief."

Poole left the establishment with a feeling of deep depression; he had been chasing a red herring and must now begin all over again. It had been a particularly neat chase, too—thanks to Inspector Bodley. He took a midday train back to Oxford and went straight to police headquarters; not a scrap of news, of any but a completely negative character, awaited him; neither did it at St. Peter's. Young Catling had disappeared completely without leaving the smallest trace of his line of departure.

It was just worthwhile, Poole thought, to interview Professor Cayzer and ascertain from him how the scrap of paper had come into Catling's possession. Teatime seemed a likely time to find the professor in his rooms and alone. Directed by the head porter, Poole made his way to the end staircase of the Old Quad and, scanning the list of names on the board, mounted to the top floor. A deep voice responded to his knock; he opened the door and walked in.

The professor, an old Norfolk jacket substituted for the regulation subfusc coat, was standing beside a table before the fire. A spirit lamp was cooking some white concoction in a saucepan, the professor stirring it from time to time, adding a few drops of liquid from a bottle. The process appeared to absorb him, as he did not look up at Poole's entry but continued to stir; a sound like a solemn chuckle suggested that he found his pastime as amusing as it was absorbing.

"I'm sorry to disturb you, sir," said Poole.

The professor looked up.

"Eh? Oh! Who are you?"

"I am Detective-Inspector Poole of Scotland Yard, sir. I was with the dean yesterday morning when you came to inquire about Mr. Catling; it was on that subject that I wanted to consult you."

As Poole spoke, it seemed to him that a sudden look of concentrated attention came into the professor's eye. It was quickly succeeded, however, by a rather meaningless smile.

"You'll forgive me if I go on with my preparations? A rather special meal for my cats. Poor Catling, yes. Poor boy—high-spirited, full of innocent fun—he will be greatly missed, Inspector. I myself shall miss him, perhaps, as much as anybody."

He broke off abruptly.

"You are employed to find him?" he asked.

"Yes, sir. I just came to ask you—"

"And you have some news of him?"

"None, sir, I'm sorry to say—there's not a trace of him anywhere. I just wanted to ask if you—"

Again the professor interrupted. He appeared to ignore the detective's attempt to question him. Blowing out the spirit lamp, he lifted the saucepan to his nose and sniffed it.

"Delicious!" he exclaimed. "Come, Inspector, I will show you my cats."

Turning abruptly, he flung open a door beyond the fireplace.

"My bedroom, really, but I have transformed it into a treasure-house."

Poole, following behind his host, found himself on the threshold of a large room fitted out as a museum. Glass cupboards lined the walls; wooden cases with glass tops stood upon the floor. The light was poor, but the detective could make out vessels of earthenware and metal, headdresses, fragments of stone and plaster covered with Egyptian figures—all the familiar treasures of the Egyptologist. The professor whisked a piece of American cloth from a glass case.

"My cats," he said.

Under the glass lay a number of mummified cats—most of them black and withered, but a few covered with fur and looking like ordinary dead cats. One form, wrapped completely in bandages, looked terribly human—like the victim of some ghastly accident. Poole felt a shudder of horror pass through him. What had the professor meant about that concoction—"for his cats"? Could it possibly be—he turned to ask a question, but found that Cayzer had left him and was standing by a sarcophagus under the window.

"My great treasure!" The professor bent over and stroked the surface of the wooden lid. "A masterpiece of the great Rameses the Second—his own process— a unique process—a usurer! The king used him to complete his experiment. The process lasted a hundred days—a hundred days—it is not complete!"

The detective had joined his host while the latter spoke. As he listened, a cold sweat broke out over his body and he felt himself tremble from head to foot. He looked at the man beside him and saw a light in his eyes—fierce, cruel, insane—that completed the terror that he felt.

With a violent effort, Poole bent down and wrenched off the lid of the sarcophagus, flinging it to the floor at one side. Inside lay what appeared to be a mummy —a human form—wrapped from head to foot, as the cat had been, in bandages, even the face being covered. Throwing a look over his shoulder, he saw the gaunt figure of the professor towering above him, one arm flung back, madness blazing from his eyes. Quick as thought, Poole flung himself downward and sideways against the professor's legs; something crashed against the wooden coffin, and the two men rolled over in a heap upon the floor.

Fortunately for Poole, the professor's head struck against the corner of one of the cases and he lay still —the detective knew well enough that he would have stood little chance against the superhuman strength of the maniac that this man must be. Rising to his feet, he bent over the sarcophagus, and with a pen-knife ripped away the bandages from the face of the

73

"mummy." As the fabric came away, there was exposed to view the white, shrunken face of a young man; the eyes were open, but the light in them was dim—they seemed barely conscious, except of unfathomable terror.

Poole rushed out on to the landing and shouted for help at the top of his voice. Two undergraduates came running up from a room below.

"Get a doctor quickly, one of you, and the police!" exclaimed the detective. "Young Catling's here— barely alive. You, come and help me!"

He dashed back into the museum—only just in time—the professor was struggling to his knees. Poole flung him back upon the floor, knelt on his shoulders, and clung to a wrist with each hand.

"Find some string or bandages and tie his ankles," he cried. "Good chap! Now his wrists—that's it—that'll do for the moment. Now help me lift this poor chap out."

Together the two men carefully lifted the bound figure from its coffin—Poole was almost glad to see that the boy had fainted—and carried it to a sofa in the sitting room. Carefully they unwound the bandages and chafed the bare, cold limbs. The boy opened his eyes and gazed wildly, uncomprehendingly, about him.

"It's all right!" said Poole cheerfully. "It's quite all right now—you're with friends!"

The eyes came to rest on his face, but instead of the relief that Poole had hoped to see in them, there came terror, dawning and growing terror. The lips moved, and Poole, putting his ear close to them, caught faintly the words: "Milk! Cement—liquid cement!"

Again the boy fainted, and at the same moment there was a clatter of feet on the stairs and a uniformed police sergeant and two constables appeared in the doorway.

"Your man's next door. Take care; he's a madman. I advise you to get an ambulance and strap him to a stretcher. Cover it with a blanket. You don't want the whole college to see what you've got. Ah, that you, Doctor? Thank heaven you've come. This poor chap's nearly out."

Poole explained what he knew of the extraordinary circumstances of the case, and it was decided that until the professor's concoction had been analyzed and perhaps an X-ray photograph taken, it was wiser not to move Catling from his present position.

Before long the boy came to his senses, and, as his color was distinctly better, he was allowed to tell his story. It was told haltingly, with many pauses and some unintelligible passages, but the gist of it was as follows:

Having accidentally come across the letter sent by the Archaeological Supply Association to Professor Cayzer, Catling had thought it would be a rag to make up as a detective and "arrest" the professor for debt. He had got himself up in his rooms on Friday afternoon after lunch and, choosing the middle of the afternoon, when everybody would be out playing games, rowing, or working, had slipped round to Old Quad, knowing well from experience that the professor always spent Friday afternoon in his rooms.

The professor had at first "risen" magnificently; he stormed and swore in the most satisfactory manner. Then he had suddenly quieted down, apparently accepting the inevitable, and offered to show the "detective" the treasures for which he was being dunned. Catling did not know whether this change implied that the professor had recognized him or not; he had followed the professor into the museum and, while looking at the mummified cats, had suddenly received a violent blow on the back of the head and had not recovered consciousness till he found himself bound as Poole had found him, except for his face, lying in the sarcophagus and the professor bending over him and explaining with ghastly glee the experiment he proposed to carry out on him.

Apparently Rameses II's process of mummification —perfected, according to legend at any rate, by experiment upon an unfortunate usurer who had angered him—consisted of the very gradual instillation into the system of the victim, while he yet lived, of some compound which gradually solidified within him; the compound contained, apparently, a preservative as well as a solidifying property, so that the mummy retained not only its shape but also its flesh. The bandages, used by the professor successfully in his experiments on cats, kept the body in its proper shape— prevented "bulging," as the madman had gleefully explained to his unfortunate victim.

In all probability the cruelty of the process had gradually affected the professor's brain and turned him from a scientific experimenter into an insane monster. In any case he never recovered his reason and was never brought to trial.

Analysis of the compound in the saucepan revealed the presence of an unknown element with some of the properties of cement, but it was in such minute percentage to the whole that there was good hope of its not having completely solidified the organs to which it adhered. This proved to be the case, and young Catling, after months of practically experimental treatment, recovered his full health. In all probability the madman's cruel desire to spin out the experiment as long as possible had saved his life.

When it was known that Catling was out of danger, Poole received an invitation from the dean to dine with him. With some trepidation he journeyed down to Oxford and found himself received especially over the "nuts and wine" in Senior Common Room after dinner as a distinguished fellow graduate of the University of Oxford.

"I knew you would prefer to be treated purely in your official capacity while the case was in hand," said Mr. Luddingham, "but I had great difficulty in not remonstrating with you when you asked me 'to approximately estimate' the amount of young Catling's debts. You must be a changed man indeed, my dear Poole—and probably a bigger one—calmly to split an infinitive in the presence of the dean of St. Peter's."

THE PROBLEM OF CELL 13

Jacques Futrelle

PRACTICALLY ALL those letters remaining in the alphabet after Augustus S. F. X. Van Dusen was named were afterward acquired by that gentleman in the course of a brilliant scientific career and, being honorably acquired, were tacked on to the other end. His name, therefore, taken with all that belonged to it, was a wonderfully imposing structure. He was a Ph.D., an LL.D., an F.R.S., an M.D., and an M.D.S. He was also some other things—just what, he himself couldn't say—through recognition of his ability by various foreign educational and scientific institutions.

In appearance he was no less striking than in nomenclature. He was slender, with the droop of the student in his thin shoulders and the pallor of a close, sedentary life on his clean-shaven face. His eyes wore a perpetual, forbidding squint—the squint of a man who studies little things—and, when they could be seen at all through his thick spectacles, were mere slits of watery blue. But above his eyes was his most striking feature. This was a tall, broad brow, almost abnormal in height and width, crowned by a heavy shock of bushy, yellow hair. All these things conspired to give him a peculiar, almost grotesque, personality.

Professor Van Dusen was remotely German. For generations his ancestors had been noted in the sciences; he was the logical result, the mastermind. First and above all he was a logician. At least thirty-five years of the half century or so of his existence had been devoted exclusively to proving that two and two always equal four, except in unusual cases, where they equal three or five, as the case may be. He stood broadly on the general proposition that all things that start must go somewhere, and was able to bring the concentrated mental force of his forefathers to bear on a given problem. Incidentally it may be remarked that Professor Van Dusen wore a number eight hat.

The world at large had heard vaguely of Professor Van Dusen as The Thinking Machine. It was a newspaper catchphrase applied to him at the time of a remarkable exhibition at chess; he had demonstrated then that a stranger to the game might, by the force of inevitable logic, defeat a champion who had devoted a lifetime to its study. The Thinking Machine! Perhaps that more nearly described him than all his honorary initials, for he spent week after week, month after month, in the seclusion of his small laboratory from which had gone forth thoughts that staggered scientific associates and deeply stirred the world at large.

It was only occasionally that The Thinking Machine

had visitors, and these were usually men who, themselves high in the sciences, dropped in to argue a point and perhaps convince themselves. Two of these men, Dr. Charles Ransome and Alfred Fielding, called one evening to discuss some theory which is not of consequence here.

"Such a thing is impossible," declared Dr. Ransome emphatically in the course of the conversation.

"Nothing is impossible," declared The Thinking Machine with equal emphasis. He always spoke petulantly. "The mind is master of all things. When science fully recognizes that fact a great advance will have been made."

"How about the airship?" asked Dr. Ransome.

"That's not impossible at all," asserted The Thinking Machine. "It will be invented sometime. I'd do it myself, but I'm busy."

Dr. Ransome laughed tolerantly.

"I've heard you say such things before," he said. "But they mean nothing. Mind may be master of matter, but it hasn't yet found a way to apply itself. There are some things that can't be *thought* out of existence, or, rather, which would not yield to any amount of thinking."

"What, for instance?" demanded The Thinking Machine.

Dr. Ransom was thoughtful for a moment as he smoked.

"Well, say prison walls," he replied. "No man can *think* himself out of a cell. If he could, there would be no prisoners."

"A man can so apply his brain and ingenuity that

81

he can leave a cell, which is the same thing," snapped
The Thinking Machine.

Dr. Ransome was slightly amused.

"Let's suppose a case," he said after a moment.
"Take a cell where prisoners under sentence of death
are confined—men who are desperate and, maddened
by fear, would take any chance to escape—suppose
you were locked in such a cell. Could you escape?"

"Certainly," declared The Thinking Machine.

"Of course," said Mr. Fielding, who entered the
conversation for the first time, "you might wreck the
cell with an explosive—but, inside, a prisoner, you
couldn't have that."

"There would be nothing of that kind," said The
Thinking Machine. "You might treat me precisely as
you treated prisoners under sentence of death, and I
would leave the cell."

"Not unless you entered it with tools prepared to
get out," said Dr. Ransome.

The Thinking Machine was visibly annoyed and
his blue eyes snapped.

"Lock me in any cell in any prison anywhere at
any time, wearing only what is necessary, and I'll
escape in a week," he declared sharply.

Dr. Ransome sat up straight in the chair, interested.
Mr. Fielding lighted a new cigar.

"You mean you could actually *think* yourself out?"
asked Dr. Ransome.

"I would get out," was the response.

"Are you serious?"

"Certainly I am serious."

Dr. Ransome and Mr. Fielding were silent for a long time.

"Would you be willing to try it?" asked Mr. Fielding finally.

"Certainly," said Professor Van Dusen, and there was a trace of irony in his voice. "I have done more asinine things than that to convince other men of less important truths."

The tone was offensive and there was an undercurrent strongly resembling anger on both sides. Of course it was an absurd thing, but Professor Van Dusen reiterated his willingness to undertake the escape and it was decided upon.

"To begin now," added Dr. Ransome.

"I'd prefer that it begin tomorrow," said The Thinking Machine, "because—"

"No, now," said Mr. Fielding flatly. "You are arrested—figuratively, of course—without any warning locked in a cell with no chance to communicate with friends, and left there with identically the same care and attention that would be given to a man under sentence of death. Are you willing?"

"All right, now, then," said The Thinking Machine, and he arose.

"Say, the death cell in Chisholm Prison."

"The death cell in Chisholm Prison."

"And what will you wear?"

"As little as possible," said The Thinking Machine. "Shoes, stockings, trousers, and a shirt."

"You will permit yourself to be searched, of course?"

"I am to be treated precisely as all prisoners are

treated," said The Thinking Machine. "No more attention and no less."

There were some preliminaries to be arranged in the matter of obtaining permission for the test, but all three were influential men and everything was done satisfactorily by telephone, albeit the prison commissioners, to whom the experiment was explained on purely scientific grounds, were sadly bewildered. Professor Van Dusen would be the most distinguished prisoner they had ever entertained.

When The Thinking Machine had donned those things which he was to wear during his incarceration, he called the little old woman who was his housekeeper, cook, and maidservant all in one.

"Martha," he said, "it is now twenty-seven minutes past nine o'clock. I am going away. One week from tonight, at half-past nine, these gentlemen and one, possibly two, others will take supper with me here. Remember, Dr. Ransome is very fond of artichokes."

The three men were driven to Chisholm Prison, where the warden was awaiting them, having been informed of the matter by telephone. He understood merely that the eminent Professor Van Dusen was to be his prisoner, if he could keep him, for one week; that he had committed no crime, but that he was to be treated as all other prisoners were treated.

"Search him," instructed Dr. Ransome.

The Thinking Machine was searched. Nothing was found on him; the pockets of the trousers were empty; the white, stiff-bosomed shirt had no pocket. The shoes and stockings were removed, examined, then replaced. As he watched all these preliminaries and noted the pitiful, childlike physical weakness of the man—the colorless face and the thin, white hands—Dr. Ransome almost regretted his part in the affair.

"Are you sure you want to do this?" he asked.

"Would you be convinced if I did not?" inquired The Thinking Machine in turn.

"No."

"All right. I'll do it."

What sympathy Dr. Ransome had was dissipated by the tone. It nettled him, and he resolved to see the experiment to the end; it would be a stinging reproof to egotism.

"It will be impossible for him to communicate with anyone outside?" he asked.

"Absolutely impossible," replied the warden. "He will not be permitted writing materials of any sort."

"And your jailers—would they deliver a message from him?"

"Not one word, directly or indirectly," said the warden. "You may rest assured of that. They will report anything he might say or turn over to me anything he might give them."

"That seems entirely satisfactory," said Mr. Fielding, who was frankly interested in the problem.

"Of course, in the event he fails," said Dr. Ransome, "and asks for his liberty, you understand you are to set him free?"

"I understand," replied the warden.

The Thinking Machine stood listening, but had nothing to say until this was all ended, then:

"I should like to make three small requests. You may grant them or not, as you wish."

"No special favors, now," warned Mr. Fielding.

"I am asking none," was the stiff response. "I should like to have some tooth powder—buy it yourself to see that it is tooth powder—and I should like to have one five-dollar and two ten-dollar bills."

Dr. Ransome, Mr. Fielding, and the warden exchanged astonished glances. They were not surprised at the request for tooth powder, but were at the request for money.

"Is there any man with whom our friend would come in contact that he could bribe with twenty-five dollars?"

"Not for twenty-five hundred dollars," was the positive reply.

"Well, let him have them," said Mr. Fielding. "I think they are harmless enough."

"And what is the third request?" asked Dr. Ransome.

"I should like to have my shoes polished."

Again the astonished glances were exchanged. This last request was the height of absurdity, so they agreed to it. These things all being attended to, The Thinking Machine was led back into the prison from which he had undertaken to escape.

"Here is Cell 13," said the warden, stopping three doors down the steel corridor. "This is where we keep condemned murderers. No one can leave it without my permission, and no one in it can communicate with the outside. I'll stake my reputation on that. It's only three doors back of my office and I can readily hear any unusual noise."

"Will this cell do, gentlemen?" asked The Thinking

Machine. There was a touch of irony in his voice.

"Admirably," was the reply.

The heavy steel door was thrown open, there was a great scurrying and scampering of tiny feet, and The Thinking Machine passed into the gloom of the cell. Then the door was closed and double-locked by the warden.

"What is that noise in there?" asked Dr. Ransome through the bars.

"Rats—dozens of them," replied The Thinking Machine tersely.

The three men, with final good nights, were turning away when The Thinking Machine called, "What time is it exactly, Warden?"

"Eleven seventeen," replied the warden.

"Thanks. I will join you gentlemen in your office at half-past eight o'clock one week from tonight," said The Thinking Machine.

"And if you do not?"

"There is no 'if' about it."

Chisholm Prison was a great, spreading structure of granite, four stories in all, which stood in the center of acres of open space. It was surrounded by a wall of solid masonry eighteen feet high and so smoothly finished inside and out as to offer no foothold to a climber, no matter how expert. Atop of this fence, as a further precaution, was a five-foot fence of steel rods, each terminating in a keen point. This fence in itself marked an absolute deadline between freedom and imprisonment, for, even if a man escaped from his cell, it would seem impossible for him to pass the wall.

The yard, which on all sides of the prison building was twenty-five feet wide, that being the distance from the building to the wall, was by day an exercise ground for those prisoners to whom was granted the boon of occasional semiliberty. But that was not for those in Cell 13. At all times of the day there were armed guards in the yard, four of them, one patrolling each side of the prison building.

By night the yard was almost as brilliantly lighted as by day. On each of the four sides was a great arc light which rose above the prison wall and gave to the guards a clear sight. The lights, too, brightly illuminated the spiked top of the wall. The wires which fed the arc lights ran up the side of the prison building on insulators and from the top story led out to the poles supporting the arc lights.

All these things were seen and comprehended by The Thinking Machine, who was only enabled to see out his closely barred cell window by standing on his bed. This was on the morning following his incarceration. He gathered, too, that the river lay over there beyond the wall somewhere, because he heard faintly the pulsation of a motorboat and high up in the air saw a river bird. From that same direction came the shouts of boys at play and the occasional crack of a batted ball. He knew then that between the prison wall and the river was an open space, a playground.

Chisholm Prison was regarded as absolutely safe. No man had ever escaped from it. The Thinking Machine, from his perch on the bed, seeing what he saw, could readily understand why. The walls of the cell, though built, he judged, twenty years before, were perfectly solid, and the window bars of new iron had not a shadow of rust on them. The window itself, even with the bars out, would be a difficult mode of egress because it was small.

Yet, seeing these things, The Thinking Machine was not discouraged. Instead, he thoughtfully squinted at the great arc light—there was bright sunlight now —and traced with his eyes the wire which led from it to the building. That electric wire, he reasoned, must come down the side of the building not a great distance from his cell. That might be worth knowing.

Cell 13 was on the same floor with the offices of the prison—that is, not in the basement, nor yet upstairs. There were only four steps up to the office floor; therefore, the level of the floor must be only three or four feet above the ground. He couldn't see the ground directly beneath his window, but he could see it further out toward the wall. It would be an easy drop from the window. Well and good.

Then The Thinking Machine fell to remembering how he had come to the cell. First there was the outside guard's booth, a part of the wall. There were two heavily barred gates there, both of steel. At this gate was one man always on guard. He admitted persons to the prison after much clanking of keys and locks and let them out when ordered to do so. The warden's office was in the prison building, and in order to reach that official from the prison yard one had to pass a gate of solid steel with only a peephole in it. Then, coming from that inner office to Cell 13, where he was now, one must pass a heavy wooden door and two steel doors into the corridors of the prison; and always there was the double-locked door of Cell 13 to reckon with.

There were, then, The Thinking Machine recalled, seven doors to be overcome before one could pass from Cell 13 into the outer world a free man. But against this was the fact that he was rarely interrupted. A jailer appeared at his cell door at six in the morning with a breakfast of prison fare; he would come again at noon and again at six in the afternoon. At nine o'clock at night would come the inspection tour. That would be all.

"It's admirably arranged, this prison system," was the mental tribute paid by The Thinking Machine. "I'll have to study it a little when I get out. I had no idea there was such great care exercised in the prisons."

There was nothing, positively nothing, in his cell except his iron bed, so firmly put together that no man could tear it to pieces save with sledges or a file. He had neither of these. There was not even a chair, or a small table, or a bit of tin or crockery. Nothing! The jailer stood by when he ate, then took away the wooden spoon and bowl which he had used.

One by one these things sank into the brain of The Thinking Machine. When the last possibility had been considered he began an examination of his cell. From the roof, down the walls on all sides, he examined the stones and the cement between them. He stamped over the floor carefully time after time, but it was cement, perfectly solid. After the examination he sat on the edge of the iron bed and was lost in thought for a long time. For Professor Augustus S. F. X. Van Dusen, The Thinking Machine, had something to think about.

He was disturbed by a rat which ran across his foot, then scampered away into a dark corner of the cell, frightened at its own daring. After a while The Thinking Machine, squinting steadily into the darkness of the corner where the rat had gone, was able to make out in the gloom many little beady eyes staring at him. He counted six pair, and there were perhaps others; he didn't see very well.

Then The Thinking Machine, from his seat on the bed, noticed for the first time the bottom of his cell door. There was an opening there of two inches between the steel bar and the floor. Still looking steadily at this opening, The Thinking Machine backed suddenly into the corner where he had seen the beady eyes. There was a great scampering of tiny feet, several squeaks of frightened rodents, and then silence.

None of the rats had gone out the door, yet there were none in the cell. Therefore there must be another way out of the cell, however small. The Thinking Machine, on hands and knees, started a search for this spot, feeling in the darkness with his long, slender fingers.

At last his search was rewarded. He came upon a small opening in the floor, level with the cement. It was perfectly round and somewhat larger than a silver dollar. This was the way the rats had gone. He put his fingers deep into the opening; it seemed to be a disused drainage pipe and was dry and dusty.

Having satisfied himself on this point, he sat on the bed again for an hour, then made another inspection of his surroundings through the small cell window. One of the outside guards stood directly opposite, beside the wall, and happened to be looking at the window of Cell 13 when the head of The Thinking Machine appeared. But the scientist didn't notice the guard.

Noon came and the jailer appeared with the prison dinner of repulsively plain food. At home The Thinking Machine merely ate to live; here he took what was offered without comment. Occasionally he spoke to the jailer who stood outside the door watching him.

"Any improvements made here in the last few years?" he asked.

"Nothing particularly," replied the jailer. "New wall was built four years ago."

"Anything done to the prison proper?"

"Painted the woodwork outside, and I believe about seven years ago a new system of plumbing was put in."

"Ah!" said the prisoner. "How far is the river over there?"

"About three hundred feet. The boys have a baseball ground between the wall and the river."

The Thinking Machine had nothing further to say just then, but when the jailer was ready to go he asked for some water.

"I get very thirsty here," he explained. "Would it be possible for you to leave a little water in a bowl for me?"

"I'll ask the warden," replied the jailer, and he went away.

Half an hour later he returned with water in a small earthen bowl.

"The warden says you may keep this bowl," he

informed the prisoner. "But you must show it to me when I ask for it. If it is broken, it will be the last."

"Thank you," said The Thinking Machine. "I shan't break it."

The jailer went on about his duties. For just the fraction of a second it seemed that The Thinking Machine wanted to ask a question, but he didn't.

Two hours later this same jailer, in passing the door of Cell number 13, heard a noise inside and stopped. The Thinking Machine was down on his hands and knees in a corner of the cell, and from that same corner came several frightened squeaks. The jailer looked on interestedly.

"Ah, I've got you," he heard the prisoner say.

"Got what?" he asked sharply.

"One of these rats," was the reply. "See?" And between the scientist's long fingers the jailer saw a small gray rat struggling. The prisoner brought it over to the light and looked at it closely.

"It's a water rat," he said.

"Ain't you got anything better to do than to catch rats?" asked the jailer.

"It's disgraceful that they should be here at all," was the irritated reply. "Take this one away and kill it. There are dozens more where it came from."

The jailer took the wriggling, squirmy rodent and flung it down on the floor violently. It gave one squeak and lay still. Later he reported the incident to the warden, who only smiled.

Still later that afternoon the outside armed guard on the Cell 13 side of the prison looked up again at the window and saw the prisoner looking out. He saw a hand raised to the barred window and then something white fluttered to the ground, directly under the window of Cell 13. It was a little roll of linen, evidently of white shirting material, and tied around it was a five-dollar bill. The guard looked up at the window again, but the face had disappeared.

With a grim smile he took the little linen roll and the five-dollar bill to the warden's office. There together they deciphered something which was written on it with a queer sort of ink, frequently blurred. On the outside was this:

Finder of this please deliver to Dr. Charles Ransome.

"Ah," said the warden with a chuckle. "Plan of escape number one has gone wrong." Then, as an afterthought: "But why did he address it to Dr. Ransome?"

"And where did he get the pen and ink to write with?" asked the guard.

The warden looked at the guard and the guard looked at the warden. There was no apparent solution of that mystery. The warden studied the writing carefully, then shook his head.

"Well, let's see what he was going to say to Dr. Ransome," he said at length, still puzzled, and he unrolled the inner piece of linen.

"Well, if that—what—what do you think of that?" he asked, dazed.

The guard took the bit of linen and read this: *"Epa cseot d'net niiy awe htto n'si sih. T."*

The warden spent an hour wondering what sort

of a cipher it was and half an hour wondering why his prisoner should attempt to communicate with Dr. Ransome, who was the cause of his being there. After this the warden devoted some thought to the question of where the prisoner got writing materials and what sort of writing materials he had. With the idea of illuminating this point, he examined the linen again. It was a torn part of a white shirt with ragged edges.

Now it was possible to account for the linen, but what the prisoner had used to write with was another matter. The warden knew it would have been impossible for him to have either pen or pencil, and, besides, neither pen nor pencil had been used in this writing. What, then? The warden decided to investigate personally. The Thinking Machine was his prisoner; he had orders to hold his prisoners; if this one sought to escape by sending cipher messages to persons outside, he would stop it, as he would have stopped it in the case of any other prisoner.

The warden went back to Cell 13 and found The Thinking Machine on his hands and knees on the floor, engaged in nothing more alarming than catching rats. The prisoner heard the warden's step and turned to him quickly.

"It's disgraceful," he snapped. "These rats. There are scores of them."

"Other men have been able to stand them," said the warden. "Here is another shirt for you—let me have the one you have on."

"Why?" demanded The Thinking Machine quickly. His tone was hardly natural; his manner suggested actual perturbation.

"You have attempted to communicate with Dr. Ransome," said the warden severely. "As my prisoner, it is my duty to put a stop to it."

The Thinking Machine was silent for a moment.

"All right," he said finally. "Do your duty."

The warden smiled grimly. The prisoner arose from the floor and removed the white shirt, putting on instead a striped convict shirt the warden had brought. The warden took the white shirt eagerly and then and there compared the pieces of linen on which was written the cipher with certain torn places in the shirt. The Thinking Machine looked on curiously.

"The guard brought *you* those, then?" he asked.

"He certainly did," replied the warden triumphantly. "And that ends your first attempt to escape."

The Thinking Machine watched the warden as he, by comparison, established to his own satisfaction that only two pieces of linen had been torn from the white shirt.

"What did you write this with?" demanded the warden.

"I should think it a part of your duty to find out," said The Thinking Machine irritably.

The warden started to say some harsh things, then restrained himself and made a minute search of the cell and of the prisoner instead. He found absolutely nothing—not even a match or toothpick which might have been used for a pen. The same mystery surrounded the fluid with which the cipher had been written. Although the warden left Cell 13 visibly annoyed, he took the torn shirt in triumph.

"Well, writing notes on a shirt won't get him out,

that's certain," he told himself with some complacency. He put the linen scraps into his desk to await developments. "If that man escapes from that cell I'll—hang it—I'll resign."

On the third day of his incarceration The Thinking Machine openly attempted to bribe his way out. The jailer had brought his dinner and was leaning against the barred door, waiting, when The Thinking Machine began the conversation.

"The drainage pipes of the prison lead to the river, don't they?" he asked.

"Yes," said the jailer.

"I suppose they are very small."

"Too small to crawl through, if that's what you're thinking about," was the grinning response.

There was silence until The Thinking Machine finished his meal. Then:

"You know I'm not a criminal, don't you?"

"Yes."

"And that I've a perfect right to be freed if I demand it?"

"Yes."

"Well, I came here believing that I could make my escape," said the prisoner, and his squint eyes studied the face of the jailer. "Would you consider a financial reward for aiding me to escape?"

The jailer, who happened to be an honest man, looked at the slender, weak figure of the prisoner, at the large head with its mass of yellow hair, and was almost sorry.

"I guess prisons like these were not built for the likes of you to get out of," he said at last.

"But would you consider a proposition to help me get out?" the prisoner insisted almost beseechingly.

"No," said the jailer shortly.

"Five hundred dollars," urged The Thinking Machine. "I am not a criminal."

"No," said the jailer.

"A thousand?"

"No," again said the jailer, and he started away hurriedly to escape further temptation. Then he turned back. "If you should give me ten thousand dollars I couldn't get you out. You'd have to pass through seven doors, and I only have the keys to two."

Then he told the warden all about it.

"Plan number two fails," said the warden, smiling grimly. "First a cipher, then bribery."

When the jailer was on his way to Cell 13 at six o'clock, again bearing food to The Thinking Machine, he paused, startled by the unmistakable scrape, scrape of steel against steel. It stopped at the sound of his steps, then craftily the jailer, who was beyond the prisoner's range of vision, resumed his tramping, the sound being apparently that of a man going away from Cell 13. As a matter of fact he was in the same spot.

After a moment there came again the steady scrape, scrape, and the jailer crept cautiously on tiptoes to the door and peered between the bars. The Thinking Machine was standing on the iron bed working at the bars of the little window. He was using a file, judging from the backward and forward swing of his arms.

Cautiously the jailer crept back to the office, summoned the warden in person, and they returned to Cell 13 on tiptoes. The steady scrape was still audible.

The warden listened to satisfy himself and then suddenly appeared at the door.

"Well?" he demanded, and there was a smile on his face.

The Thinking Machine glanced back from his perch on the bed and leaped suddenly to the floor, making frantic efforts to hide something. The warden went in with hand extended.

"Give it up," he said.

"No," said the prisoner sharply.

"Come, give it up," urged the warden. "I don't want to have to search you again."

"No," repeated the prisoner.

"What was it—a file?" asked the warden.

The Thinking Machine was silent and stood squinting at the warden with something very nearly approaching disappointment on his face—nearly, but not quite. The warden was almost sympathetic.

"Plan number three fails, eh?" he asked good-naturedly. "Too bad, isn't it?"

The prisoner didn't say.

"Search him," instructed the warden.

The jailer searched the prisoner carefully. At last, artfully concealed in the waistband of the trousers, he found a piece of steel about two inches long, with one side curved like a half-moon.

"Ah," said the warden as he received it from the jailer. "From your shoe heel." He smiled pleasantly.

The jailer continued his search and on the other side of the trousers waistband found another piece of steel identical with the first. The edges showed where they had been worn against the bars of the window.

"You couldn't saw a way through those bars with these," said the warden.

"I could have," said The Thinking Machine firmly.

"In six months, perhaps," said the warden good-naturedly.

The warden shook his head slowly as he gazed into the slightly flushed face of his prisoner.

"Ready to give it up?" he asked.

"I haven't started yet," was the prompt reply.

Then came another exhaustive search of the cell. Carefully the two men went over it, finally turning out the bed and searching that. Nothing. The warden in person climbed upon the bed and examined the bars of the window where the prisoner had been sawing. When he looked he was amused.

"Just made it a little bright by hard rubbing," he said to the prisoner, who stood looking on with a somewhat crestfallen air. The warden grasped the iron bars in his strong hands and tried to shake them. They were immovable, set firmly in the solid granite. He examined each in turn and found them all satisfactory. Finally he climbed down from the bed.

"Give it up, Professor," he advised.

The Thinking Machine shook his head and the warden and jailer passed on again. As they disappeared down the corridor The Thinking Machine sat on the edge of the bed with his head in his hands.

"He's crazy to try to get out of that cell," commented the jailer.

"Of course he can't get out," said the warden. "But he's clever. I would like to know what he wrote that cipher with."

101

It was four o'clock next morning when an awful, heart-racking shriek of terror resounded through the great prison. It came from a cell, somewhere about the center, and its tone told a tale of horror, agony, terrible fear. The warden heard and with three of his men rushed into the long corridor leading to Cell 13.

As they ran there came again that awful cry. It died away in a sort of wail. The white faces of prisoners appeared at cell doors upstairs and down, staring out wonderingly, frightened.

"It's that fool in Cell 13," grumbled the warden.

He stopped and stared in as one of the jailers flashed a lantern. "That fool in Cell 13" lay comfortably on his cot, flat on his back with his mouth open, snoring. Even as they looked there came again the piercing cry from somewhere above. The warden's face blanched a little as he started up the stairs. There on the top floor he found a man in Cell 43, directly above Cell 13 but two floors higher, cowering in a corner of his cell.

"What's the matter?" demanded the warden.

"Thank God you've come," exclaimed the prisoner, and he cast himself against the bars of his cell.

"What is it?" demanded the warden again.

He threw open the door and went in. The prisoner dropped on his knees and clasped the warden about the body. His face was white with terror, his eyes were widely distended, and he was shuddering. His hands, icy cold, clutched at the warden's.

"Take me out of this cell; please take me out," he pleaded.

"What's the matter with you, anyhow?" insisted the warden impatiently.

"I heard something—something," said the prisoner, and his eyes roved nervously around the cell.

"What did you hear?"

"I—I can't tell you," stammered the prisoner. Then, in a sudden burst of terror: "Take me out of this cell —put me anywhere—but take me out of here."

The warden and the three jailers exchanged glances.

"Who is this fellow? What's he accused of?" asked the warden.

"Joseph Ballard," said one of the jailers. "He's accused of throwing acid in a woman's face. She died from it."

"But they can't prove it," gasped the prisoner. "They can't prove it. Please put me in some other cell."

He was still clinging to the warden, and that official threw his arms off roughly. Then for a time he stood looking at the cowering wretch, who seemed possessed of all the wild, unreasoning terror of a child.

"Look here, Ballard," said the warden finally, "if you heard anything, I want to know what it was. Now tell me."

"I can't, I can't," was the reply. He was sobbing.

"Where did it come from?"

"I don't know. Everywhere—nowhere. I just heard it."

"What was it—a voice?"

"Please don't make me answer," pleaded the prisoner.

"You must answer," said the warden sharply.

"It was a voice—but—but it wasn't human," was the sobbing reply.

"Voice, but not human?" repeated the warden, puzzled.

"It sounded muffled and—and far away—and ghostly," explained the man.

"Did it come from inside or outside the prison?"

"It didn't seem to come from anywhere—it was just here, here, everywhere. I heard it. I heard it."

For an hour the warden tried to get the story, but Ballard had become suddenly obstinate and would say nothing—only pleaded to be placed in another cell or to have one of the jailers remain near him until daylight. These requests were gruffly refused.

"And see here," said the warden in conclusion, "if there's any more of this screaming I'll put you in the padded cell."

Then the warden went his way, a sadly puzzled man. Ballard sat at his cell door until daylight, his face, drawn and white with terror, pressed against the bars, and looked out into the prison with wide, staring eyes.

That day, the fourth since the incarceration of The Thinking Machine, was enlivened considerably by the volunteer prisoner, who spent most of his time at the little window of his cell. He began proceedings by throwing another piece of linen down to the guard, who picked it up dutifully and took it to the warden. On it was written: "Only three days more."

The warden was in no way surprised at what he read; he understood that The Thinking Machine meant only three days more of his imprisonment, and he regarded the note as a boast. But how was the thing written? Where had The Thinking Machine found this new piece of linen? Where? How? He carefully examined the linen. It was white, of fine texture, shirting material. He took the shirt which he had taken and carefully fitted the two original pieces of the linen to the torn places. This third piece was entirely superfluous; it didn't fit anywhere, and yet it was unmistakably the same goods.

"And where—where does he get anything to write with?" demanded the warden of the world at large.

Still later on the fourth day The Thinking Machine, through the window of his cell, spoke to the armed guard outside.

"What day of the month is it?" he asked.

"The fifteenth," was the answer.

The Thinking Machine made a mental astronomical calculation and satisfied himself that the moon would not rise until after nine o'clock that night. Then he asked another question:

"Who attends to those arc lights?"

"Man from the company."

"You have no electricians in the building?"

"No."

"I should think you could save money if you had your own man."

"None of my business," replied the guard.

The guard noticed The Thinking Machine at the cell window frequently during that day, but always the face seemed listless and there was a certain wistfulness in the squint eyes behind the glasses. After a while he accepted the presence of the leonine head as a matter of course. He had seen other prisoners do the same thing; it was the longing for the outside world.

That afternoon, just before the day guard was relieved, the head appeared at the window again, and The Thinking Machine's hand held something out between the bars. It fluttered to the ground and the guard picked it up. It was a five-dollar bill.

"That's for you," called the prisoner.

As usual, the guard took it to the warden. That gentleman looked at it suspiciously; he looked at everything that came from Cell 13 with suspicion.

"He said it was for me," explained the guard.

"It's a sort of a tip, I suppose," said the warden. "I see no particular reason why you shouldn't accept—"

Suddenly he stopped. He had remembered that The Thinking Machine had gone into Cell 13 with one five-dollar bill and two ten-dollar bills—twenty-five dollars in all. Now, a five-dollar bill had been tied around the first piece of linen that came from the cell. The warden still had it, and to convince himself he took it out and looked at it. It was five dollars; yet here was another five dollars, and The Thinking Machine had only had ten-dollar bills.

"Perhaps somebody changed one of the bills for him," he thought at last with a sigh of relief.

But then and there he made up his mind. He would search Cell 13 as a cell was never before searched in this world. When a man could write at will, and change money, and do other wholly inexplicable things, there was something radically wrong with his prison. He planned to enter the cell at night—three o'clock would be an excellent time. The Thinking Machine must do all the weird things he did sometime. Night seemed the most reasonable.

Thus it happened that the warden stealthily descended upon Cell 13 that night at three o'clock. He paused at the door and listened. There was no sound save the steady, regular breathing of the prisoner. The keys unfastened the double locks with scarcely a clank, and the warden entered, locking the door behind him. Suddenly he flashed his dark lantern in the face of the recumbent figure.

If the warden had planned to startle The Thinking Machine he was mistaken, for that individual merely opened his eyes quietly, reached for his glasses, and inquired in a most matter-of-fact tone, "Who is it?"

It would be useless to describe the search that the warden made. It was minute. Not one inch of the cell or the bed was overlooked. He found the round hole in the floor and, with a flash of inspiration, thrust his thick fingers into it. After a moment of fumbling there he drew up something and looked at it in the light of his lantern.

"Ugh!" he exclaimed.

The thing he had taken out was a rat—a dead rat. His inspiration fled as a mist before the sun. But he continued the search. The Thinking Machine, without a word, arose and kicked the rat out of the cell into the corridor.

The warden climbed on the bed and tried the steel bars in the tiny window. They were perfectly rigid; every bar of the door was the same.

Then the warden searched the prisoner's clothing,

beginning at the shoes. Nothing hidden in them! Then the trousers waistband. Still nothing! Then the pockets of the trousers. From one side he drew out some paper money and examined it.

"Five one-dollar bills," he gasped.

"That's right," said the prisoner.

"But the—you had two tens and a five—what the —how do you do it?"

"That's my business," said the Thinking Machine.

"Did any of my men change this money for you— on your word of honor?"

The Thinking Machine paused just a fraction of a second.

"No," he said.

"Well, do you make it?" asked the warden. He was prepared to believe anything.

"That's my business," again said the prisoner.

The warden glared at the eminent scientist fiercely. He felt—he knew—that this man was making a fool of him, yet he didn't know how. If he were a real prisoner he would get the truth—but then perhaps those inexplicable things which had happened would not have been brought before him so sharply. Neither of the men spoke for a long time, then suddenly the warden turned fiercely and left the cell, slamming the door behind him. He didn't dare to speak then.

He glanced at the clock. It was ten minutes to four. He had hardly settled himself in bed when again came that heartbreaking shriek through the prison. With a few muttered words, which, while not elegant, were highly expressive, he relighted his lantern and rushed through the prison again to the cell on the upper floor.

Again Ballard was crushing himself against the steel door, shrieking, shrieking at the top of his voice. He stopped only when the warden flashed his lamp in the cell.

"Take me out; take me out," he screamed. "I did it—I did it—I killed her. Take it away."

"Take what away?" asked the warden.

"I threw the acid in her face—I did it—I confess. Take me out of here."

Ballard's condition was pitiable; it was only an act of mercy to let him out into the corridor. There he crouched in a corner like an animal at bay and clasped his hands to his ears. It took half an hour to calm him sufficiently for him to speak. Then he told incoherently what had happened. On the night before at four o'clock he had heard a voice—a sepulchral voice, muffled and wailing in tone.

"What did it say?" asked the warden curiously.

"Acid—acid—acid!" gasped the prisoner. "It accused me. Acid! I threw the acid, and the woman died. Oh!" It was a long, shuddering wail of terror.

"Acid?" echoed the warden, puzzled. The case was beyond him.

"Acid. That's all I heard—that one word, repeated several times. There were other things, too, but I didn't hear them."

"That was last night, eh?" asked the warden. "What happened tonight—what frightened you just now?"

"It was the same thing," gasped the prisoner. "Acid—acid—acid!" He covered his face with his hands and sat shivering. "It was acid I used on her, but I didn't mean to kill her. I just heard the words. It was something accusing me—accusing me." He mumbled and was silent.

"Did you hear anything else?"

"Yes—but I couldn't understand—only a little bit —just a word or two."

"Well, what was it?"

"I heard 'acid' three times, then I heard a long, moaning sound, then—then—I heard 'number eight hat.' I heard that twice."

"Number eight hat," repeated the warden. "What the devil—number eight hat? Accusing voices of conscience have never talked about number eight hats, so far as I ever heard."

"He's insane," said one of the jailers with an air of finality.

"I believe you," said the warden. "He must be. He probably heard something and got frightened. He's trembling now. Number eight hat! What the—"

When the fifth day of The Thinking Machine's imprisonment rolled around, the warden was wearing a hunted look. He was anxious for the end of the thing. He could not help but feel that his distinguished prisoner had been amusing himself. And if this were so, The Thinking Machine had lost none of his sense of humor. For on this fifth day he flung down another linen note to the outside guard, bearing the words: "Only two days more." Also he flung down half a dollar.

Now the warden knew—he *knew*—that the man in Cell 13 didn't have any half-dollars—he *couldn't* have any half-dollars, no more than he could have pen and ink and linen, and yet he did have them. It was a condition, not a theory; that is one reason why the warden was wearing a hunted look.

That ghastly, uncanny thing, too, about "acid" and "number eight hat" clung to him tenaciously. They didn't mean anything, of course—merely the ravings of an insane murderer who had been driven by fear to confess his crime—still, there were so many things that "didn't mean anything" happening in the prison now since The Thinking Machine was there.

On the sixth day the warden received a letter stating that Dr. Ransome and Mr. Fielding would be at Chisholm Prison on the following evening, Thursday, and in the event Professor Van Dusen had not yet escaped —and they presumed he had not because they had not heard from him—they would meet him there.

"In the event he has not yet escaped!" The warden smiled grimly. *Escaped!*

The Thinking Machine enlivened this day for the warden with three notes. They were on the usual linen and bore generally on the appointment at half-past eight o'clock Thursday night, which appointment the scientist had made at the time of his imprisonment.

On the afternoon of the seventh day the warden passed Cell 13 and glanced in. The Thinking Machine was lying on the iron bed, apparently sleeping lightly. The cell appeared precisely as it always did from a casual glance. The warden would swear that no man was going to leave it between that hour—it was then four o'clock—and half-past eight o'clock that evening.

On his way back past the cell the warden heard the steady breathing again and, coming close to the door, looked in. He wouldn't have done so if The Thinking Machine had been looking, but now—well, it was different.

A ray of light came through the high window and fell on the face of the sleeping man. It occurred to the warden for the first time that his prisoner appeared haggard and weary. Just then The Thinking Machine stirred slightly and the warden hurried on up the corridor guiltily. That evening after six o'clock he saw the jailer.

"Everything all right in Cell 13?" he asked.

"Yes, sir," replied the jailer. "He didn't eat much, though."

It was with a feeling of having done his duty that the warden received Dr. Ransome and Mr. Fielding shortly after seven o'clock. He intended to show them the linen notes and lay before them the full story of his woes, which was a long one. But before this came to pass the guard from the river side of the prison yard entered the office.

"The arc light in my side of the yard won't light," he informed the warden.

"Confound it, that man's a hoodoo," thundered the official. "Everything has happened since he's been here."

The guard went back to his post in the darkness, and the warden phoned to the electric light company.

"This is Chisholm Prison," he said through the phone. "Send three or four men down here quick to fix an arc light."

The reply was evidently satisfactory, for the warden hung up the receiver and passed out into the yard.

While Dr. Ransome and Mr. Fielding sat waiting, the guard at the outer gate came in with a special delivery letter. Dr. Ransome happened to notice the address and, when the guard went out, looked at the letter more closely.

"By George!" he exclaimed.

"What is it?" asked Mr. Fielding.

Silently the doctor offered the letter. Mr. Fielding examined it closely.

"Coincidence," he said. "It must be."

It was nearly eight o'clock when the warden returned to his office. The electricians had arrived in a wagon and were now at work. The warden pressed the buzz-button communicating with the man at the outer gate in the wall.

"How many electricians came in?" he asked over the short phone. "Four? Three workmen in jumpers and overalls and the manager? Frock coat and silk hat? All right. Be certain that only four go out. That's all."

He turned to Dr. Ransome and Mr. Fielding.

"We have to be careful here—particularly"—and there was broad sarcasm in his tone—"since we have scientists locked up."

The warden picked up the special delivery letter carelessly and then began to open it.

"When I read this I want to tell you gentlemen something about how—great Caesar!" he ended suddenly as he glanced at the letter. He sat with mouth open, motionless from astonishment.

"What is it?" asked Mr. Fielding.

"A special delivery letter from Cell 13," gasped the

warden. "An invitation to supper."

"What?" And the two others arose unanimously.

The warden sat dazed, staring at the letter for a moment, then called sharply to a guard outside in the corridor.

"Run down to Cell 13 and see if that man's in there."

The guard went as directed, while Dr. Ransome and Mr. Fielding examined the letter.

"It's Van Dusen's handwriting; there's no question of that," said Dr. Ransome. "I've seen too much of it."

Just then the buzz on the telephone from the outer gate sounded, and the warden, in a semitrance, picked up the receiver.

"Hello! Two reporters, eh? Let 'em come in." He turned suddenly to the doctor and Mr. Fielding. "Why, the man *can't* be out. He must be in his cell."

Just at that moment the guard returned.

"He's still in his cell, sir," he reported. "I saw him. He's lying down."

"There, I told you so," said the warden, and he breathed freely again. "But how did he mail that letter?"

There was a rap on the steel door which led from the jailyard into the warden's office.

"It's the reporters," said the warden. "Let them in," he instructed the guard. Then to the two other gentlemen: "Don't say anything about this before them, because I'd never hear the last of it."

The door opened, and the two men from the front gate entered.

"Good evening, gentlemen," said one. That was Hutchinson Hatch; the warden knew him well.

"Well?" demanded the other irritably. "I'm here."

That was The Thinking Machine.

He squinted belligerently at the warden, who sat with mouth agape. For the moment that official had nothing to say. Dr. Ransome and Mr. Fielding were amazed, but they didn't know what the warden knew. They were only amazed; he was paralyzed. Hutchinson Hatch, the reporter, took in the scene with greedy eyes.

"How—how—how did you do it?" gasped the warden finally.

"Come back to the cell," said The Thinking Machine in the irritated voice which his scientific associates knew so well.

The warden, still in a condition bordering on trance, led the way.

"Flash your light in there," directed The Thinking Machine.

The warden did so. There was nothing unusual in the appearance of the cell, and there—there on the bed lay the figure of The Thinking Machine. Certainly! There was the yellow hair! Again the warden looked at the man beside him and wondered at the strangeness of his own dreams.

With trembling hands he unlocked the cell door and The Thinking Machine passed inside.

"See here," he said.

He kicked at the steel bars in the bottom of the cell door and three of them were pushed out of place. A fourth broke off and rolled away in the corridor.

"And here, too," directed the erstwhile prisoner as he stood on the bed to reach the small window. He

swept his hand across the opening and every bar came out.

"What's this in bed?" demanded the warden, who was slowly recovering.

"A wig," was the reply. "Turn down the cover."

The warden did so. Beneath it lay a large coil of strong rope, thirty feet or more; a dagger; three files; ten feet of electric wire; a thin, powerful pair of steel pliers; a small tack hammer with its handle; and— and a derringer pistol.

"How did you do it?" demanded the warden.

"You gentlemen have an engagement to supper with me at half-past nine o'clock," said The Thinking Machine. "Come on, or we shall be late."

"But how did you do it?" insisted the warden.

"Don't ever think you can hold any man who can use his brain," said The Thinking Machine. "Come on; we shall be late."

It was an impatient supper party in the rooms of Professor Van Dusen, and a somewhat silent one. The guests were Dr. Ransome; Alfred Fielding; the warden; and Hutchinson Hatch, reporter. The meal was served to the minute, in accordance with Professor Van Dusen's instructions of one week before; Dr. Ransome found the artichokes delicious. At last the supper was finished and The Thinking Machine turned full on Dr. Ransome and squinted at him fiercely.

"Do you believe it now?" he demanded.

"I do," replied Dr. Ransome.

"Do you admit that it was a fair test?"

"I do."

With the others, particularly the warden, he was waiting anxiously for the explanation.

"Suppose you tell us how—" began Mr. Fielding.

"Yes, tell us how," said the warden.

The Thinking Machine readjusted his glasses, took a couple of preparatory squints at his audience, and began the story. He told it from the beginning logically, and no man ever talked to more interested listeners.

"My agreement was," he began, "to go into a cell, carrying nothing except what was necessary to wear, and to leave that cell within a week. I had never seen Chisholm Prison. When I went into the cell I asked for tooth powder, two ten- and one five-dollar bills, and also to have my shoes blacked. Even if these requests had been refused it would not have mattered seriously. But you agreed to them.

"I knew there would be nothing in the cell which you thought I might use to advantage. So when the warden locked the door on me I was apparently helpless, unless I could turn three seemingly innocent things to use. They were things which would have been permitted any prisoner under sentence of death, were they not, Warden?"

"Tooth powder and polished shoes, yes, but not money," replied the warden.

"Anything is dangerous in the hands of a man who knows how to use it," went on The Thinking Machine. "I did nothing that first night but sleep and chase rats." He glared at the warden. "When the matter was broached I knew I could do nothing that night, so suggested next day. You gentlemen thought I wanted

118

time to arrange an escape with outside assistance, but this was not true. I knew I could communicate with whom I pleased, when I pleased."

The warden stared at him a moment, then went on smoking solemnly.

"I was aroused next morning at six o'clock by the jailer with my breakfast," continued the scientist. "He told me dinner was at twelve and supper at six. Between these times, I gathered, I would be pretty much to myself. So immediately after breakfast I examined my outside surroundings from my cell window. One look told me it would be useless to try to scale the wall, even should I decide to leave my cell by the window, for my purpose was to leave not only the cell, but the prison. Of course, I could have gone over the wall, but it would have taken me longer to lay my plans that way. Therefore, for the moment, I dismissed all idea of that.

"From this first observation I knew the river was on that side of the prison and that there was also a playground there. Subsequently these surmises were verified by a keeper. I knew then one important thing —that anyone might approach the prison wall from that side if necessary without attracting any particular attention. That was well to remember. I remembered it.

"But the outside thing which most attracted my attention was the feed wire to the arc light which ran within a few feet—probably three or four—of my cell window. I knew that would be valuable in the event I found it necessary to cut off that arc light."

"Oh, you shut it off, then?" asked the warden.

"Having learned all I could from that window," resumed The Thinking Machine without heeding the interruption, "I considered the idea of escaping through the prison proper. I recalled just how I had come into the cell, which I knew would be the only way. Seven doors lay between me and the outside. So, also for the time being, I gave up the idea of escaping that way. And I couldn't go through the solid granite walls of the cell."

The Thinking Machine paused for a moment and Dr. Ransome lighted a new cigar. For several minutes there was silence, then the scientific jailbreaker went on:

"While I was thinking about these things a rat ran across my foot. It suggested a new line of thought. There were at least half a dozen rats in the cell—I could see their beady eyes. Yet I had noticed none come under the cell door. I frightened them purposely and watched the cell door to see if they went out that way. They did not, but they were gone. Obviously they went another way. Another way meant another opening.

"I searched for this opening and found it. It was an old drainpipe, long unused and partly choked with dirt and dust. But this was the way the rats had come. They came from somewhere. Where? Drainpipes usually lead outside prison grounds. This one probably led to the river or near it. The rats must therefore come from that direction. If they came a part of the way, I reasoned that they came all the way, because it was extremely unlikely that a solid iron or lead pipe would have any hole in it except at the exit.

"When the jailer came with my luncheon he told me two important things, although he didn't know it. One was that a new system of plumbing had been put in the prison seven years before; another that the river was only three hundred feet away. Then I knew positively that the pipe was a part of an old system; I knew, too, that it slanted generally toward the river. But did the pipe end in the water or on land?

"This was the next question to be decided. I decided it by catching several of the rats in the cell. My jailer was surprised to see me engaged in this work. I examined at least a dozen of them. They were perfectly dry; they had come through the pipe, and, most important of all, they were *not house rats, but field rats*. The other end of the pipe was on land, then, outside the prison walls. So far, so good.

"Then I knew that if I worked freely from this point I must attract the warden's attention in another direction. You see, by telling the warden that I had come there to escape you made the test more severe, because I had to trick him by false scents."

The warden looked up with a sad expression in his eyes.

"The first thing was to make him think I was trying to communicate with you, Dr. Ransome. So I wrote a note on a piece of linen I tore from my shirt, addressed it to Dr. Ransome, tied a five-dollar bill around it, and threw it out the window. I knew the guard would take it to the warden, but I rather hoped the warden would send it as addressed. Have you that first linen note, Warden?"

The warden produced the cipher.

"What the deuce does it mean, anyhow?" he asked.

"Read it backward, beginning with the 'T' signature and disregard the division into words," instructed The Thinking Machine.

The warden did so.

"*T-h-i-s,* this," he spelled, studied it a moment, then read it off, grinning. "This is not the way I intend to escape.

"Well, now, what do you think o' that?" he demanded, still grinning.

"I knew that would attract your attention, just as it did," said The Thinking Machine, "and if you really found out what it was it would be a sort of gentle rebuke."

"What did you write it with?" asked Dr. Ransome after he had examined the linen and passed it to Mr. Fielding.

"This," said the erstwhile prisoner, and he extended his foot. On it was the shoe he had worn in prison, though the polish was gone—scraped off clean. "The shoe blacking, moistened with water, was my ink; the metal tip of the shoelace made a fairly good pen."

The warden looked up and suddenly burst into a laugh, half of relief, half of amusement.

"You're a wonder," he said admiringly. "Go on."

"That precipitated a search of my cell by the warden, as I had intended," continued The Thinking Machine. "I was anxious to get the warden into the habit of searching my cell, so that finally, constantly finding nothing, he would get disgusted and quit. This at last happened, practically."

The warden blushed.

"He then took my white shirt away and gave me a prison shirt. He was satisfied that those two pieces of the shirt were all that was missing. But while he was searching my cell I had another piece of that same shirt, about nine inches square, rolled into a small ball in my mouth."

"Nine inches of that shirt?" demanded the warden. "Where did it come from?"

"The bosoms of all stiff white shirts are of triple thickness," was the explanation. "I tore out the inside thickness, leaving the bosom only two thicknesses. I knew you wouldn't see it. So much for that."

There was a little pause, and the warden looked from one to another of the men with a sheepish grin.

"Having disposed of the warden for the time being by giving him something else to think about, I took my first serious step toward freedom," said Professor Van Dusen. "I knew, within reason, that the pipe led somewhere to the playground outside; I knew a great many boys played there; I knew that rats came into my cell from out there. Could I communicate with someone outside with these things at hand?

"First was necessary, I saw, a long and fairly reliable thread, so—but here." He pulled up his trousers legs and showed that the tops of both stockings, of fine, strong lisle, were gone. "I unraveled those—after I got them started it wasn't difficult—and I had easily a quarter of a mile of thread that I could depend on.

"Then on half of my remaining linen I wrote, laboriously enough, I assure you, a letter explaining my situation to this gentleman here." And he indicated Hutchinson Hatch. "I knew he would assist me—for the value of the newspaper story. I tied firmly to this linen letter a ten-dollar bill—there is no surer way of attracting the eye of anyone—and wrote on the linen: 'Finder of this deliver to Hutchinson Hatch, *Daily American,* who will give another ten dollars for the information.'

"The next thing was to get this note outside on that playground where a boy might find it. There were two ways, but I chose the best. I took one of the rats—I became adept in catching them—tied the linen and money firmly to one leg, fastened my lisle thread to another, and turned him loose in the drainpipe. I reasoned that the natural fright of the rodent would make him run until he was outside the pipe, and then out on earth he would probably stop to gnaw off the linen and money.

"From the moment the rat disappeared into that dusty pipe I became anxious. I was taking so many chances. The rat might gnaw the string, of which I held one end; other rats might gnaw it; the rat might run out of the pipe and leave the linen and money where they would never be found; a thousand other things might have happened. So began some nervous hours, but the fact that the rat ran on until only a few feet of the string remained in my cell made me think he was outside the pipe. I had carefully instructed Mr. Hatch what to do in case the note reached him. The question was: Would it reach him?

"This done, I could only wait and make other plans in case this one failed. I openly attempted to bribe my jailer and learned from him that he held the keys to only two of seven doors between me and freedom.

Then I did something else to make the warden nervous. I took the steel supports out of the heels of my shoes and made a pretense of sawing the bars of my cell window. The warden raised a pretty row about that. He developed, too, the habit of shaking the bars of my cell window to see if they were solid. They were— then."

Again the warden grinned. He had ceased being astonished.

"With this one plan I had done all I could and could only wait to see what happened," the scientist went on. "I couldn't know whether my note had been delivered or even found, or whether the rat had gnawed it up. And I didn't dare to draw back through the pipe that one slender thread which connected me with the outside.

"When I went to bed that night I didn't sleep for fear there would come the slight signal twitch at the thread which was to tell me that Mr. Hatch had received the note. At half-past three o'clock, I judge, I felt this twitch, and no prisoner actually under sentence of death ever welcomed a thing more heartily."

The Thinking Machine stopped and turned to the reporter.

"You'd better explain just what you did," he said.

"The linen note was brought to me by a small boy who had been playing baseball," said Mr. Hatch. "I immediately saw a big story in it, so I gave the boy another ten dollars and got several spools of silk, some twine, and a roll of light, pliable wire. The professor's note suggested that I have the finder of the note show me just where it was picked up and told me to make my search from there, beginning at two o'clock in the morning. If I found the other end of the thread I was to twitch it gently three times, then a fourth.

"I began the search with a small-bulb electric light. It was an hour and twenty minutes before I found the end of the drainpipe, half-hidden in weeds. The pipe was very large there, say twelve inches across. Then I found the end of the lisle thread, twitched it as directed, and immediately I got an answering twitch.

"Then I fastened the silk to this and Professor Van Dusen began to pull it into his cell. I nearly had heart disease for fear the string would break. To the end of the silk I fastened the twine, and when that had been pulled in I tied on the wire. Then that was drawn into the pipe and we had a substantial line, which rats couldn't gnaw, from the mouth of the drain into the cell."

The Thinking Machine raised his hand and Hatch stopped.

"All this was done in absolute silence," said the scientist. "But when the wire reached my hand I could have shouted. Then we tried another experiment, which Mr. Hatch was prepared for. I tested the pipe as a speaking tube. Neither of us could hear very clearly, but I dared not speak loud for fear of attracting attention in the prison. At last I made him understand what I wanted immediately. He seemed to have great difficulty in understanding when I asked for nitric acid, and I repeated the word 'acid' several times.

"Then I heard a shriek from a cell above me. I knew instantly that someone had overheard, and when I heard you coming, Mr. Warden, I feigned sleep. If you had entered my cell at that moment that whole plan of escape would have ended there. But you passed on. That was the nearest I ever came to being caught.

"Having established this improvised trolley, it is easy to see how I got things in the cell and made them disappear at will. I merely dropped them back into the pipe. You, Mr. Warden, could not have reached the connecting wire with your fingers; they are too large. My fingers, you see, are longer and more slender. In addition, I guarded the top of that pipe with a rat —you remember how."

"I remember," said the warden with a grimace.

"I thought that if anyone were tempted to investigate that hole the rat would dampen his ardor. Mr. Hatch could not send me anything useful through the pipe until next night, although he did send me change for ten dollars as a test, so I proceeded with other parts of my plan. Then I evolved the method of escape which I finally employed.

"In order to carry this out successfully it was necessary for the guard in the yard to get accustomed to seeing me at the cell window. I arranged this by dropping linen notes to him, boastful in tone, to make the warden believe, if possible, one of his assistants was communicating with the outside for me. I would stand at my window for hours gazing out, so the guard could see, and occasionally I spoke to him. In that way I learned that the prison had no electricians of its own, but was dependent upon the light company if anything should go wrong.

"That cleared the way to freedom perfectly. Early in the evening of the last day of my imprisonment, when it was dark, I planned to cut the feed wire, which was only a few feet from my window, reaching it with an acid-tipped wire I had. That would make that side of the prison perfectly dark while the electricians were searching for the break. That would also bring Mr. Hatch into the prison yard.

"There was only one more thing to do before I actually began the work of setting myself free. This was to arrange final details with Mr. Hatch through our speaking tube. I did this within half an hour after the warden left my cell on the fourth night of my imprisonment. Mr. Hatch again had serious difficulty in understanding me, and I repeated the word 'acid' to him several times and later on the words 'number eight hat'—that's my size—and these were the things which made a prisoner upstairs confess to murder, so one of the jailers told me next day. This prisoner heard our voices—confused, of course—through the pipe, which also went to his cell. The cell directly over me was not occupied, hence no one else heard.

"Of course, the actual work of cutting the steel bars out of the window and door was comparatively easy with nitric acid, which I got through the pipe in tin bottles, but it took time. Hour after hour on the fifth and sixth and seventh days the guard below was looking at me as I worked on the bars of the window with the acid on a piece of wire. I used the tooth powder to prevent the acid from spreading. I looked away abstractedly as I worked and each minute the acid cut deeper into the metal. I noticed that the jailers always tried the door by shaking the upper part, never the lower bars; therefore I cut the lower bars, leaving them hanging in place by thin strips of metal. But that was a bit of daredeviltry. I could not have gone that way so easily."

The Thinking Machine sat silent for several minutes.

"I think that makes everything clear," he went on. "Whatever points I have not explained were merely to confuse the warden and jailers. These things in my bed I brought in to please Mr. Hatch, who wanted to improve the story. Of course, the wig was necessary in my plan. The special delivery letter I wrote and directed in my cell with Mr. Hatch's fountain pen, then sent it out to him, and he mailed it. That's all, I think."

"But your actually leaving the prison grounds and then coming in through the outer gate to my office?" asked the warden.

"Perfectly simple," said the scientist. "I cut the electric light wire with acid, as I said, when the current was off. Therefore when the current was turned on, the arc didn't light. I knew it would take some time to find out what was the matter and make repairs. When the guard went to report to you the yard was dark, I crept out the window—it was a tight fit, too—replaced the bars by standing on a narrow ledge, and remained in a shadow until the force of electricians arrived. Mr. Hatch was one of them.

"When I saw him I spoke and he handed me a cap, a jumper, and overalls, which I put on within ten feet of you, Mr. Warden, while you were in the yard. Later Mr. Hatch called me, presumably as a workman, and together we went out the gate to get something out of the wagon. The gate guard let us pass out readily as two workmen who had just passed in. We changed our clothing and reappeared, asking to see you. We saw you. That's all."

There was silence for several minutes. Dr. Ransome was first to speak.

"Wonderful!" he exclaimed. "Perfectly amazing."

"How did Mr. Hatch happen to come with the electricians?" asked Mr. Fielding.

"His father is manager of the company," replied The Thinking Machine.

"But what if there had been no Mr. Hatch outside to help?"

"Every prisoner has one friend outside who would help him escape if he could."

"Suppose—just suppose—there had been no old plumbing system there?" asked the warden curiously.

"There were two other ways out," said The Thinking Machine enigmatically.

Ten minutes later the telephone bell rang. It was a request for the warden.

"Light all right, eh?" the warden asked through the phone. "Good. Wire cut beside Cell 13? Yes, I know. One electrician too many? What's that? Two came out?"

The warden turned to the others with a puzzled expression.

"He only let in four electricians, he has let out two, and says there are three left."

"I was the odd one," said The Thinking Machine.

"Oh," said the warden. "I see." Then through the phone: "Let the fifth man go. He's all right."

SILVER BLAZE

A. Conan Doyle

I AM AFRAID, Watson, that I shall have to go," said Holmes as we sat down together to our breakfast one morning.

"Go! Where to?"

"To Dartmoor; to King's Pyland."

I was not surprised. Indeed, my only wonder was that he had not already been mixed up in this extraordinary case which was the one topic of conversation through the length and breadth of England. For a whole day my companion had rambled about the room with his chin upon his chest and his brows knitted, charging and recharging his pipe with the strongest black tobacco, and absolutely deaf to any of my questions or remarks. Fresh editions of every paper had been sent up by our news agent, only to be glanced over and tossed down into a corner. Yet, silent as he was, I knew perfectly well what it was over which he was brooding. There was but one problem before the public which could challenge his powers of analysis, and that was the singular disappearance of the favorite for the Wessex Cup and the tragic murder of its trainer. When, therefore, he suddenly announced his intention of setting out for the scene of the drama, it was only what I had both expected and hoped for.

"I should be most happy to go down with you if I should not be in the way," said I.

"My dear Watson, you would confer a great favor upon me by coming. And I think that your time will not be misspent, for there are points about the case which promise to make it an absolutely unique one. We have, I think, just time to catch our train at Paddington, and I will go further into the matter upon our journey. You would oblige me by bringing with you your very excellent field glass?"

And so it happened that an hour or so later I found myself in the corner of a first-class carriage flying along en route for Exeter, while Sherlock Holmes, with his sharp, eager face framed in his ear-flapped traveling cap, dipped rapidly into the bundle of fresh papers which he had procured at Paddington. We had left Reading far behind us before he thrust the last one of them under the seat and offered me his cigar case.

"We are going well," said he, looking out of the window and glancing at his watch. "Our rate at present is fifty-three and a half miles an hour."

"I have not observed the quarter-mile posts," said I.

"Nor have I. But the telegraph posts upon this line are sixty yards apart, and the calculation is a simple one. I presume that you have looked into this matter of the murder of John Straker and the disappearance of Silver Blaze?"

"I have seen what the *Telegraph* and the *Chronicle* have to say."

"It is one of those cases where the art of the reasoner should be used rather for the sifting of details than for the acquiring of fresh evidence. The tragedy has been so uncommon, so complete, and of such personal importance to so many people that we are suffering from a plethora of surmise, conjecture, and hypothesis. The difficulty is to detach the framework of fact— of absolute, undeniable fact—from the embellishments of theorists and reporters. Then, having established ourselves upon this sound basis, it is our duty to see what inferences may be drawn and what are the special points upon which the whole mystery turns. On Tuesday evening I received telegrams from both Colonel Ross, the owner of the horse, and from Inspector Gregory, who is looking after the case, inviting my cooperation."

"Tuesday evening!" I exclaimed. "And this is Thursday morning. Why didn't you go down yesterday?"

"Because I made a blunder, my dear Watson—which is, I am afraid, a more common occurrence than anyone would think who only knew me through your memoirs. The fact is that I could not believe it possible that the most remarkable horse in England could long remain concealed, especially in so sparsely inhabited a place as the north of Dartmoor. From hour to hour yesterday I expected to hear that he had been found and that his abductor was the murderer of John

Straker. When, however, another morning had come and I found that beyond the arrest of young Fitzroy Simpson nothing had been done, I felt that it was time for me to take action. Yet in some ways I feel that yesterday has not been wasted."

"You have formed a theory, then?"

"At least I have got a grip of the essential facts of the case. I shall enumerate them to you, for nothing clears up a case so much as stating it to another person, and I can hardly expect your cooperation if I do not show you the position from which we start."

I lay back against the cushions, puffing at my cigar, while Holmes, leaning forward, with his long, thin forefinger checking off the points upon the palm of his left hand, gave me a sketch of the events which had led to our journey.

"Silver Blaze," said he, "is from the Somomy stock and holds as brilliant a record as his famous ancestor. He is now in his fifth year and has brought in turn each of the prizes of the turf to Colonel Ross, his fortunate owner. Up to the time of the catastrophe he was the first favorite for the Wessex Cup, the betting being three to one on him. He has always, however, been a prime favorite with the racing public and has never yet disappointed them, so that even at those odds enormous sums of money have been laid upon him. It is obvious, therefore, that there were many people who had the strongest interest in preventing Silver Blaze from being there at the fall of the flag next Tuesday.

"The fact was, of course, appreciated at King's Pyland, where the colonel's training stable is situated.

Every precaution was taken to guard the favorite. The trainer, John Straker, is a retired jockey who rode in Colonel Ross's colors before he became too heavy for the weighing chair. He has served the colonel for five years as jockey and for seven as trainer, and has always shown himself to be a zealous and honest servant. Under him were three lads, for the establishment was a small one, containing only four horses in all. One of these lads sat up each night in the stable, while the others slept in the loft. All three bore excellent characters. John Straker, who is a married man, lived in a small villa about two hundred yards from the stables. He has no children, keeps one maidservant, and is comfortably off. The country round is very lonely, but about half a mile to the north there is a small cluster of villas which have been built by a Tavistock contractor for the use of invalids and others who may wish to enjoy the Dartmoor air. Tavistock itself lies two miles to the west, while across the moor, also about two miles distant, is the larger training establishment of Mapleton, which belongs to Lord Backwater and is managed by Silas Brown. In every other direction the moor is a complete wilderness, inhabited only by a few roaming gypsies. Such was the general situation last Monday night when the catastrophe occurred.

"On that evening the horses had been exercised and watered as usual, and the stables were locked up at nine o'clock. Two of the lads walked up to the trainer's house, where they had supper in the kitchen, while the third, Ned Hunter, remained on guard. At a few minutes after nine the maid, Edith Baxter, carried down to the stables his supper, which consisted of a dish of curried mutton. She took no liquid, as there was a water tap in the stables, and it was the rule that the lad on duty should drink nothing else. The maid carried a lantern with her, as it was very dark and the path ran across the open moor.

"Edith Baxter was within thirty yards of the stables when a man appeared out of the darkness and called to her to stop. As he stepped into the circle of yellow light thrown by the lantern she saw that he was a person of gentlemanly bearing, dressed in a gray suit of tweeds with a cloth cap. He wore gaiters and carried a heavy stick with a knob to it. She was most impressed, however, by the extreme pallor of his face and by the nervousness of his manner. His age, she thought, would be rather over thirty than under it.

" 'Can you tell me where I am?' he asked. 'I had almost made up my mind to sleep on the moor when I saw the light of your lantern.'

" 'You are close to the King's Pyland training stables,' said she.

" 'Oh, indeed! What a stroke of luck!' he cried. 'I understand that a stable boy sleeps there alone every night. Perhaps that is his supper which you are carrying to him. Now, I am sure that you would not be too proud to earn the price of a new dress, would you?' He took a piece of white paper folded up out of his waistcoat pocket. 'See that the boy has this tonight, and you shall have the prettiest frock that money can buy.'

"She was frightened by the earnestness of his manner and ran past him to the window through which she was accustomed to hand the meals. It was already opened, and Hunter was seated at the small table inside. She had begun to tell him of what had happened when the stranger came up again.

" 'Good evening,' he said, looking through the window. 'I wanted to have a word with you.' The girl has sworn that as he spoke she noticed the corner of the little paper packet protruding from his closed hand.

" 'What business have you here?' asked the lad.

" 'It's business that may put something into your pocket,' said the other. 'You've two horses in for the Wessex Cup—Silver Blaze and Bayard. Let me have the straight tip and you won't be a loser. Is it a fact that at the weights Bayard could give the other a hundred yards in five furlongs, and that the stable have put their money on him?'

" 'So, you're one of those touts!' cried the lad. 'I'll show you how we serve them in King's Pyland.' He sprang up and rushed across the stable to unloose the dog. The girl fled away to the house, but as she ran she looked back and saw that the stranger was leaning through the window. A minute later, however, when Hunter rushed out with the hound he was gone, and though he ran all round the buildings he failed to find any trace of him."

"One moment," I asked. "Did the stable boy, when he ran out with the dog, leave the door unlocked behind him?"

"Excellent, Watson, excellent!" murmured my companion. "The importance of the point struck me so forcibly that I sent a special wire to Dartmoor yesterday to clear the matter up. The boy locked the door before he left it. The window, I may add, was not large

137

enough for a man to get through.

"Hunter waited until his fellow grooms had returned, when he sent a message to the trainer and told him what had occurred. Straker was excited at hearing the account, although he does not seem to have quite realized its true significance. It left him, however, vaguely uneasy, and Mrs. Straker, waking at one in the morning, found that he was dressing. In reply to her inquiries, he said that he could not sleep on account of his anxiety about the horses and that he intended to walk down to the stables to see that all was well. She begged him to remain at home, as she could hear the rain pattering against the window, but in spite of her entreaties he pulled on his large mackintosh and left the house.

"Mrs. Straker awoke at seven in the morning to find that her husband had not yet returned. She dressed herself hastily, called the maid, and set off for the stables. The door was open; inside, huddled together upon a chair, Hunter was sunk in a state of absolute stupor, the favorite's stall was empty, and there were no signs of his trainer.

"The two lads who slept in the chaff-cutting loft above the harness room were quickly aroused. They had heard nothing during the night, for they are both sound sleepers. Hunter was obviously under the influence of some powerful drug, and as no sense could be got out of him, he was left to sleep it off while the two lads and the two women ran out in search of the absentees. They still had hopes that the trainer had for some reason taken out the horse for early exercise, but on ascending the knoll near the house, not only could see no signs of the missing favorite, but they perceived something which warned them that they were in the presence of a tragedy.

"About a quarter of a mile from the stables John Straker's overcoat was flapping from a furze bush. Immediately beyond there was a bowl-shaped depression in the moor, and at the bottom of this was found the dead body of the unfortunate trainer. His head had been shattered by a savage blow from some heavy weapon, and he was wounded on the thigh, where there was a long, clean cut, inflicted evidently by some very sharp instrument. It was clear, however, that Straker had defended himself vigorously against his assailants, for in his right hand he held a small knife which was clotted with blood up to the handle, while in his left he clasped a red and black silk cravat, which was recognized by the maid as having been worn on the preceding evening by the stranger who had visited the stables. Hunter, on recovering from his stupor, was also quite positive as to the ownership of the cravat. He was equally certain that the same stranger had, while standing at the window, drugged his curried mutton and so deprived the stables of their watchman. As to the missing horse, there were abundant proofs in the mud which lay at the bottom of the fatal hollow that he had been there at the time of the struggle. But from that morning he has disappeared, and although a large reward has been offered and all the gypsies of Dartmoor are on the alert, no news has come of him. Finally, an analysis has shown that the remains of the supper left by the stable lad contained an appreciable quantity of powdered opium, while the people at the house partook of the same dish on the same night without any ill effect.

"Those are the main facts of the case, stripped of all surmise and stated as baldly as possible. I shall now recapitulate what the police have done in the matter.

"Inspector Gregory, to whom the case has been committed, is an extremely competent officer. Were he but gifted with imagination he might rise to great heights in his profession. On his arrival he promptly found and arrested the man upon whom suspicion naturally rested. There was little difficulty in finding him, for he inhabited one of those villas which I have mentioned. His name, it appears, was Fitzroy Simpson. He was a man of excellent birth and education who had squandered a fortune upon the turf and who lived now by doing a little quiet and genteel bookmaking in the sporting clubs of London. An examination of his betting book shows that bets to the amount of five thousand pounds had been registered by him against the favorite. On being arrested, he volunteered a statement that he had come down to Dartmoor in the hope of getting some information about the King's Pyland horses and also about Desborough, the second favorite, which was in charge of Silas Brown at the Mapleton stables. He did not attempt to deny that he had acted as described upon the evening before, but declared that he had no sinister designs and had simply wished to obtain firsthand information. When confronted with his cravat, he turned very pale and was utterly unable to account for its presence in the hand of the murdered man. His wet clothing showed that he had been out in the storm of the night before, and his stick, which was a penang-lawyer weighted with lead, was just such a weapon as might, by repeated blows, have inflicted the terrible injuries to which the trainer had succumbed. On the other hand, there was no wound upon his person, while the state of Straker's knife would show that one at least of his assailants must bear his mark upon him. There you have it all in a nutshell, Watson, and if you can give me any light I shall be infinitely obliged to you."

I had listened with the greatest interest to the statement which Holmes, with characteristic clearness, had laid before me. Though most of the facts were familiar to me, I had not sufficiently appreciated their relative importance nor their connection to each other.

"Is it not possible," I suggested, "that the incised wound upon Straker may have been caused by his own knife in the convulsive struggles which follow any brain injury?"

"It is more than possible; it is probable," said Holmes. "In that case, one of the main points in favor of the accused disappears."

"And yet," said I, "even now I fail to understand what the theory of the police can be."

"I am afraid that whatever theory we state has very grave objections to it," returned my companion. "The police imagine, I take it, that this Fitzroy Simpson, having drugged the lad and having in some way obtained a duplicate key, opened the stable door and took out the horse, with the intention, apparently, of kidnapping him altogether. His bridle is missing, so that Simpson must have put this on. Then, having left the door open behind him, he was leading the horse away over the moor when he was either met or overtaken by the trainer. A row naturally ensued. Simpson beat out the trainer's brains with his heavy stick without receiving any injury from the small knife which Straker used in self-defense, and then the thief either led the horse on to some secret hiding place, or else it may have bolted during the struggle and be now wandering out on the moors. That is the case as it appears to the police, and, improbable as it is, all other explanations are more improbable still. However, I shall very quickly test the matter when I am once upon the spot, and until then I cannot really see how we can get much further than our present position."

It was evening before we reached the little town of Tavistock, which lies, like the boss of a shield, in the middle of the huge circle of Dartmoor. Two gentlemen were awaiting us in the station—the one a tall, fair man with lionlike hair and beard and curiously penetrating light blue eyes; the other a small, alert person, very neat and dapper in a frock coat and gaiters, with trim little side whiskers and an eyeglass. The latter was Colonel Ross, the well-known sportsman; the other, Inspector Gregory, a man who was rapidly making his name in the detective service.

"I am delighted that you have come down, Mr. Holmes," said the colonel. "The inspector here has done all that could possibly be suggested, but I wish to leave no stone unturned in trying to avenge poor Straker and in recovering my horse."

"Have there been any fresh developments?" asked Holmes.

"I am sorry to say that we have made very little progress," said the inspector. "We have an open carriage outside, and as you would no doubt like to see the place before the light fails, we might talk it over as we drive."

A minute later we were all seated in a comfortable landau and were rattling through the quaint old Devonshire city. Inspector Gregory was full of his case and poured out a stream of remarks, while Holmes threw in an occasional question or interjection. Colonel Ross leaned back with his arms folded and his hat tilted over his eyes while I listened with interest to the dialogue of the two detectives. Gregory was formulating his theory, which was almost exactly what Holmes had foretold in the train.

"The net is drawn pretty close round Fitzroy Simpson," he remarked, "and I believe myself that he is our man. At the same time, I recognize that the evidence is purely circumstantial, and that some new development may upset it."

"How about Straker's knife?"

"We have quite come to the conclusion that he wounded himself in his fall."

"My friend Dr. Watson made that suggestion to me as we came down. If so, it would tell against this man Simpson."

"Undoubtedly. He has neither a knife nor any sign of a wound. The evidence against him is certainly very strong. He had a great interest in the disappearance of the favorite. He lies under suspicion of having poisoned the stable boy, he was undoubtedly out in the storm, he was armed with a heavy stick, and his cravat

144

was found in the dead man's hand. I really think we have enough to go before a jury."

Holmes shook his head. "A clever counsel would tear it all to rags," said he. "Why should he take the horse out of the stable? If he wished to injure it, why could he not do it there? Has a duplicate key been found in his possession? What chemist sold him the powdered opium? Above all, where could he, a stranger to the district, hide a horse—and such a horse as this? What is his own explanation as to the paper which he wished the maid to give to the stable boy?"

"He says that it was a ten-pound note. One was found in his purse. But your other difficulties are not so formidable as they seem. He is not a stranger to the district. He has twice lodged at Tavistock in the summer. The opium was probably brought from London. The key, having served its purpose, would be hurled away. The horse may be at the bottom of one of the pits or old mines upon the moor."

"What does he say about the cravat?"

"He acknowledges that it is his and declares that he had lost it. But a new element has been introduced into the case which may account for his leading the horse from the stable."

Holmes pricked up his ears.

"We have found traces which show that a party of gypsies encamped on Monday night within a mile of the spot where the murder took place. On Tuesday they were gone. Now, presuming that there was some understanding between Simpson and these gypsies, might he not have been taking them the horse when he was overtaken, and may they not have him now?"

"It is certainly possible."

"The moor is being scoured for these gypsies. I have also examined every stable and outbuilding in Tavistock and for a radius of ten miles."

"There is another training stable quite close, I understand?"

"Yes, and that is a factor which we must certainly not neglect. As Desborough, their horse, was second in the betting, they had an interest in the disappearance of the favorite. Silas Brown, the trainer, is known to have had large bets upon the event, and he was no friend to poor Straker. We have, however, examined the stables, and there is nothing to connect him with the affair."

"And nothing to connect this man Simpson with the interests of the Mapleton stables?"

"Nothing at all."

Holmes leaned back in the carriage, and the conversation ceased. A few minutes later our driver pulled up at a neat little red brick villa with overhanging eaves which stood by the road. Some distance off, across a paddock, lay a long gray-tiled outbuilding. In every other direction the low curves of the moor, bronze-colored from the fading ferns, stretched away to the skyline, broken only by the steeples of Tavistock and by a cluster of houses away to the westward which marked the Mapleton stables. We all sprang out with the exception of Holmes, who continued to lean back with his eyes fixed upon the sky in front of him, entirely absorbed in his own thoughts. It was only when I touched his arm that he roused himself with a violent start and stepped out of the carriage.

"Excuse me," said he, turning to Colonel Ross, who had looked at him in some surprise. "I was daydreaming." There was a gleam in his eyes and a suppressed excitement in his manner which convinced me, used as I was to his ways, that his hand was upon a clue, though I could not imagine where he had found it.

"Perhaps you would prefer at once to go on to the scene of the crime, Mr. Holmes?" said Gregory.

"I think that I should prefer to stay here a little and go into one or two questions of detail. Straker was brought back here, I presume?"

"Yes, he lies upstairs. The inquest is tomorrow."

"He has been in your service some years, Colonel Ross?"

"I have always found him an excellent servant."

"I presume that you made an inventory of what he had in his pockets at the time of his death, Inspector?"

"I have the things themselves in the sitting room if you would care to see them."

"I should be very glad."

We all filed into the front room and sat round the central table while the inspector unlocked a square tin box and laid a small heap of things before us. There was a box of vestas, two inches of tallow candle, an ADP brierroot pipe, a pouch of sealskin with half an ounce of long-cut Cavendish, a silver watch with a gold chain, five sovereigns in gold, an aluminum pencil case, a few papers, and an ivory-handled knife with a very delicate, inflexible blade marked WEISS & CO., LONDON.

"This is a very singular knife," said Holmes, lifting

it up and examining it minutely. "I presume, as I see bloodstains upon it, that it is the same one which was found in the dead man's grasp. Watson, this knife is surely in your line?"

"It is what we call a cataract knife," said I.

"I thought so. A very delicate blade devised for very delicate work. A strange thing for a man to carry with him upon a rough expedition, especially as it would not shut in his pocket."

"The tip was guarded by a disc of cork which we found beside his body," said the inspector. "His wife tells us that the knife had lain upon the dressing table, and that he had picked it up as he left the room. It was a poor weapon but perhaps the best that he could lay his hands on at the moment."

"Very possibly. How about these papers?"

"Three of them are receipted hay dealers' accounts. One of them is a letter of instructions from Colonel Ross. This other is a milliner's account for thirty-seven pounds fifteen made out by Madame Lesurier, of Bond Street, to William Derbyshire. Mrs. Straker tells us that Derbyshire was a friend of her husband's and that occasionally his letters were addressed here."

"Madame Derbyshire had somewhat expensive tastes," remarked Holmes, glancing down the account. "Twenty-two guineas is rather heavy for a single costume. However, there appears to be nothing more to learn, and we may now go down to the scene of the crime."

As we emerged from the sitting room a woman who had been waiting in the passage took a step forward and laid her hand upon the inspector's sleeve. Her face was haggard and thin and eager, stamped with the print of a recent horror.

"Have you got them? Have you found them?" she panted.

"No, Mrs. Straker. But Mr. Holmes here has come from London to help us, and we shall do all that is possible."

"Surely I met you in Plymouth at a garden party some little time ago, Mrs. Straker?" said Holmes.

"No, sir; you are mistaken."

"Dear me! Why, I could have sworn to it. You wore a costume of dove-colored silk with ostrich-feather trimming."

"I never had such a dress, sir," answered the lady.

"Ah, that quite settles it," said Holmes. And with an apology he followed the inspector outside. A short walk across the moor took us to the hollow in which the body had been found. At the brink of it was the furze bush upon which the coat had been hung.

"There was no wind that night, I understand," said Holmes.

"None, but very heavy rain."

"In that case, the overcoat was not blown against the furze bush but placed there."

"Yes, it was laid across the bush."

"You fill me with interest. I perceive that the ground has been trampled up a good deal. No doubt many feet have been here since Monday night."

"A piece of matting has been laid here at the side, and we have all stood upon that."

"Excellent."

"In this bag I have one of the boots which Straker

wore, one of Fitzroy Simpson's shoes, and a cast horse-shoe of Silver Blaze."

"My dear Inspector, you surpass yourself!" Holmes took the bag, and, descending into the hollow, he pushed the matting into a more central position. Then, stretching himself upon his face and leaning his chin upon his hands, he made a careful study of the trampled mud in front of him. "Hullo!" said he suddenly. "What's this?" It was a wax vesta, half-burned, which was so coated with mud that it looked at first like a little chip of wood.

"I cannot think how I came to overlook it," said the inspector with an expression of annoyance.

"It was invisible, buried in the mud. I only saw it because I was looking for it."

"What! You expected to find it?"

"I thought it not unlikely."

He took the boots from the bag and compared the impressions of each of them with marks upon the ground. Then he clambered up to the rim of the hollow and crawled about among the ferns and bushes.

"I am afraid that there are no more tracks," said the inspector. "I have examined the ground very carefully for a hundred yards in each direction."

"Indeed!" said Holmes, rising. "I should not have the impertinence to do it again after what you say. But I should like to take a little walk over the moor before it grows dark that I may know my ground tomorrow, and I think that I shall put this horseshoe into my pocket for luck."

Colonel Ross, who had shown some signs of impatience at my companion's quiet and systematic method of work, glanced at his watch. "I wish you would come back with me, Inspector," said he. "There are several points on which I should like your advice, especially as to whether we do not owe it to the public to remove our horse's name from the entries for the cup."

"Certainly not," cried Holmes with decision. "I should let the name stand."

The colonel bowed. "I am very glad to have had your opinion, sir," said he. "You will find us at poor Straker's house when you have finished your walk, and we can drive together into Tavistock."

He turned back with the inspector, while Holmes and I walked slowly across the moor. The sun was beginning to sink behind the stable of Mapleton, and the long, sloping plain in front of us was tinged with gold, deepening into rich, ruddy browns where the faded ferns and brambles caught the evening light. But the glories of the landscape were all wasted upon my companion, who was sunk in the deepest thought.

"It's this way, Watson," said he at last. "We may leave the question of who killed John Straker for the instant and confine ourselves to finding out what has become of the horse. Now, supposing that he broke away during or after the tragedy—where could he have gone to? The horse is a very gregarious creature. If left to himself his instincts would have been either to return to King's Pyland or go over to Mapleton. Why should he run wild upon the moor? He would surely have been seen by now. And why should gypsies kidnap him? These people always clear out when they hear of trouble, for they do not wish to be pestered by the police. They could not hope to sell such a horse. They would run a great risk and gain nothing by taking him. Surely that is clear."

"Where is he, then?"

"I have already said that he must have gone to King's Pyland or to Mapleton. He is not at King's Pyland. Therefore he is at Mapleton. Let us take that as a working hypothesis and see what it leads us to. This part of the moor, as the inspector remarked, is very hard and dry. But it falls away toward Mapleton, and you can see from here that there is a long hollow over yonder, which must have been very wet on Monday night. If our supposition is correct, then the horse must have crossed that, and there is the point where we should look for his tracks."

We had been walking briskly during this conversation and a few more minutes brought us to the hollow in question. At Holmes's request I walked down the bank to the right, and he to the left, but I had not taken fifty paces before I heard him give a shout and saw him waving his hand to me. The track of a horse was plainly outlined in the soft earth in front of him, and the shoe which he took from his pocket exactly fitted the impression.

"See the value of imagination," said Holmes. "It is the one quality which Gregory lacks. We imagined what might have happened, acted upon the supposition, and find ourselves justified. Let us proceed."

We crossed the marshy bottom and passed over a quarter of a mile of dry, hard turf. Again the ground sloped, and again we came on the tracks. Then we lost them for half a mile, but only to pick them up once more quite close to Mapleton. It was Holmes who saw them first, and he stood pointing with a look of triumph upon his face. A man's track was visible beside the horse's.

"The horse was alone before," I cried.

"Quite so. It was alone before. Hullo, what is this?"

The double track turned sharply off and took the direction of King's Pyland. Holmes whistled, and we both followed along after it. His eyes were on the trail, but I happened to look a little to one side and saw to my surprise the same tracks coming back again in the opposite direction.

"One for you, Watson," said Holmes when I pointed it out. "You have saved us a long walk, which would have brought us back on our own traces. Let us follow the return track."

We had not to go far. It ended at the paving of asphalt which led up to the gates of the Mapleton stables. As we approached, a groom ran out from them.

"We don't want any loiterers about here," said he.

"I only wished to ask a question," said Holmes, with his finger and thumb in his waistcoat pocket. "Should I be too early to see your master, Mr. Silas Brown, if I were to call at five o'clock tomorrow morning?"

"Bless you, sir, if anyone is about he will be, for he is always the first stirring. But here he is, sir, to answer your questions for himself. No, sir, no, it is as much as my place is worth to let him see me touch your money. Afterward, if you like."

As Sherlock Holmes replaced the half crown which

he had drawn from his pocket, a fierce-looking elderly man strode out from the gate with a hunting crop swinging in his hand.

"What's this, Dawson?" he cried. "No gossiping! Go about your business! And you, what the devil do you want here?"

"Ten minutes' talk with you, my good sir," said Holmes in the sweetest of voices.

"I've no time to talk to every gadabout. We want no strangers here. Be off or you may find a dog at your heels."

Holmes leaned forward and whispered something in the trainer's ear. He started violently and flushed to the temples.

"It's a lie!" he shouted. "An infernal lie!"

"Very good. Shall we argue about it here in public or talk it over in your parlor?"

"Oh, come in if you wish to."

Holmes smiled. "I shall not keep you more than a few minutes, Watson," said he. "Now, Mr. Brown, I am quite at your disposal."

It was twenty minutes, and the reds had all faded into grays before Holmes and the trainer reappeared. Never have I seen such a change as had been brought about in Silas Brown in that short time. His face was ashy pale, beads of perspiration shone upon his brow, and his hands shook until the hunting crop wagged like a branch in the wind. His bullying, overbearing manner was all gone, too, and he cringed along at my companion's side like a dog with its master.

"Your instructions will be done. It shall all be done," said he.

"There must be no mistake," said Holmes, looking round at him. The other winced as he read the menace in his eyes.

"Oh, no, there shall be no mistake. It shall be there. Should I change it first or not?"

Holmes thought a little and then burst out laughing. "No, don't," said he. "I shall write to you about it. No tricks, now, or—"

"Oh, you can trust me, you can trust me!"

"Yes, I think I can. Well, you shall hear from me tomorrow." He turned upon his heel, disregarding the trembling hand which the other held out to him, and we set off for King's Pyland.

"A more perfect compound of the bully, coward, and sneak than Master Silas Brown I have seldom met with," remarked Holmes as we trudged along together.

"He has the horse, then?"

"He tried to bluster out of it, but I described to him so exactly what his actions had been upon that morning that he is convinced that I was watching him. Of course you observed the peculiarly square toes in the impressions and that his own boots exactly corresponded to them. Again, of course no subordinate would have dared to do such a thing. I described to him how, when according to his custom he was the first down, he perceived a strange horse wandering over the moor. How he went out to it, and his astonishment at recognizing—from the white forehead which has given the favorite its name—that chance had put in his power the only horse which could beat the one upon which he had put his money. Then I described how his first impulse had been to lead him back to

King's Pyland, and how the devil had shown him how he could hide the horse until the race was over, and how he had led it back and concealed it at Mapleton. When I told him every detail he gave it up and thought only of saving his own skin."

"But his stables had been searched?"

"Oh, an old horse-faker like him has many a dodge."

"But are you not afraid to leave the horse in his power now, since he has every interest in injuring it?"

"My dear fellow, he will guard it as the apple of his eye. He knows that his only hope of mercy is to produce it safe."

"Colonel Ross did not impress me as a man who would be likely to show much mercy in any case."

"The matter does not rest with Colonel Ross. I follow my own methods and tell as much or as little as I choose. That is the advantage of being unofficial. I don't know whether you observed it, Watson, but the colonel's manner has been just a trifle cavalier to me. I am inclined now to have a little amusement at his expense. Say nothing to him about the horse."

"Certainly not without your permission."

"And of course this is all quite a minor point compared to the question of who killed John Straker."

"And you will devote yourself to that?"

"On the contrary, we both go back to London by the night train."

I was thunderstruck by my friend's words. We had only been a few hours in Devonshire, and that he should give up an investigation which he had begun so brilliantly was quite incomprehensible to me. Not a word more could I draw from him until we were back at the trainer's house. The colonel and the inspector were awaiting us in the parlor.

"My friend and I return to town by the night express," said Holmes. "We have had a charming little breath of your beautiful Dartmoor air."

The inspector opened his eyes, and the colonel's lip curled in a sneer.

"So you despair of arresting the murderer of poor Straker," said he.

Holmes shrugged his shoulders. "There are certainly grave difficulties in the way," said he. "I have every hope, however, that your horse will start upon Tuesday, and I beg that you will have your jockey in readiness. Might I ask for a photograph of Mr. John Straker?"

The inspector took one from an envelope and handed it to him. .

"My dear Gregory, you anticipate all my wants. If I might ask you to wait here for an instant, I have a question which I should like to put to the maid."

"I must say that I am rather disappointed in our London consultant," said Colonel Ross bluntly as my friend left the room. "I do not see that we are any further than when he came."

"At least you have his assurance that your horse will run," said I.

"Yes, I have his assurance," said the colonel with a shrug. "I should prefer to have the horse."

I was about to make some reply in defense of my friend when he entered the room again.

"Now, gentlemen," said he, "I am quite ready for Tavistock."

As we stepped into the carriage one of the stable lads held the door open for us. A sudden idea seemed to occur to Holmes, for he leaned forward and touched the lad upon the sleeve.

"You have a few sheep in the paddock," he said. "Who attends to them?"

"I do, sir."

"Have you noticed anything amiss with them of late?"

"Well, sir, not of much account, but three of them have gone lame, sir."

I could see that Holmes was extremely pleased, for he chuckled and rubbed his hands together.

"A long shot, Watson, a very long shot," said he, pinching my arm. "Gregory, let me recommend to your attention this singular epidemic among the sheep. Drive on, coachman!"

Colonel Ross still wore an expression which showed the poor opinion which he had formed of my companion's ability, but I saw by the inspector's face that his attention had been keenly aroused.

"You consider that to be important?" he asked.

"Exceedingly so."

"Is there any point to which you would wish to draw my attention?"

"To the curious incident of the dog in the nighttime."

"The dog did nothing in the nighttime."

"That was the curious incident," remarked Holmes.

Four days later Holmes and I were again in the train, bound for Winchester to see the race for the

Wessex Cup. Colonel Ross met us by appointment outside the station, and we drove in his drag to the course beyond the town. His face was grave and his manner cold in the extreme.

"I have seen nothing of my horse," said he.

"I suppose that you would know him when you saw him?" asked Holmes.

The colonel was very angry. "I have been on the turf for twenty years and never was asked such a question as that before," said he. "A child would know Silver Blaze with his white forehead and his mottled off-foreleg."

"How is the betting?"

"Well, that is the curious part of it. You could have got fifteen to one yesterday, but the price has become shorter and shorter, until you can hardly get three to one now."

"Hum!" said Holmes. "Somebody knows something, that is clear."

As the drag drew up in the enclosure near the grand-stand I glanced at the card to see the entries:

Wessex Plate [it ran] 50 sovs. each h ft with 1000 sovs. added, for four- and five-year-olds. Second £300. Third £200. New course (one mile and five furlongs).

1. Mr. Heath Newton's The Negro. Red cap. Cinnamon jacket.
2. Colonel Wardlaw's Pugilist. Pink cap. Blue and black jacket.
3. Lord Backwater's Desborough. Yellow cap and sleeves.

4. Colonel Ross's Silver Blaze. Black cap. Red jacket.
5. Duke of Balmoral's Iris. Yellow and black stripes.
6. Lord Singleford's Rasper. Purple cap. Black sleeves.

"We scratched our other one and put all hopes on your word," said the colonel. "Why, what is that? Silver Blaze favorite?"

"Five to four against Silver Blaze!" roared the ring. "Five to four against Silver Blaze! Five to fifteen against Desborough! Five to four on the field!"

"There are the numbers up," I cried. "They are all six there."

"All six there? Then my horse is running," cried the colonel in great agitation. "But I don't see him. My colors have not passed."

"Only five have passed. This must be he."

As I spoke, a powerful bay horse swept out from the weighing enclosure and cantered past us, bearing on its back the well-known black and red of the colonel.

"That's not my horse," cried the owner. "That beast has not a white hair upon its body. What is this that you have done, Mr. Holmes?"

"Well, well, let us see how he gets on," said my friend imperturbably. For a few minutes he gazed through my field glass. "Capital! An excellent start!" he cried. "There they are, coming round the curve!"

From our drag we had a superb view as they came up the straight. The six horses were so close together

that a carpet covered them, but halfway up the yellow of the Mapleton stable showed to the front. Before they reached us, however, Desborough's bolt was shot, and the colonel's horse, coming away with a rush, passed the post a good six lengths before its rival, the Duke of Balmoral's Iris making a bad third.

"It's my race, anyhow," gasped the colonel, passing his hand over his eyes. "I confess that I can make neither head nor tail of it. Don't you think that you have kept up your mystery long enough, Mr. Holmes?"

"Certainly, Colonel, you shall know everything. Let us all go round and have a look at the horse together. Here he is," he continued as we made our way into the weighing enclosure where only owners and their friends find admittance. "You have only to wash his face and his leg in spirits of wine, and you will find that he is the same old Silver Blaze as ever."

"You take my breath away."

"I found him in the hands of a faker and took the liberty of running him just as he was sent over."

"My dear sir, you have done wonders. The horse looks very fit and well. It never went better in its life. I owe you a thousand apologies for having doubted your ability. You have done me a great service by recovering my horse. You would do me a greater service still if you could lay your hands on the murderer of John Straker."

"I have done so," said Holmes quietly.

The colonel and I stared at him in amazement. "You have got him! Where is he, then?"

"He is here!"

"Here! Where?"

"In my company at the present moment."

The colonel flushed angrily. "I quite recognize that I am under obligations to you, Mr. Holmes," said he, "but I must regard what you have just said as either a very bad joke or an insult."

Sherlock Holmes laughed. "I assure you that I have not associated you with the crime, Colonel," said he. "The real murderer is standing immediately behind you." He stepped past and laid his hand upon the glossy neck of the thoroughbred.

"The horse!" cried both the colonel and myself.

"Yes, the horse. And it may lessen his guilt if I say that it was done in self-defense, and that John Straker was a man who was entirely unworthy of your confidence. But there goes the bell, and as I stand to win a little on this next race, I shall defer a lengthy explanation until a more fitting time."

We had the corner of a Pullman car to ourselves that evening as we whirled back to London, and I fancy that the journey was a short one to Colonel Ross as well as to myself as we listened to our companion's narrative of the events which had occurred at the Dartmoor training stables upon that Monday night and the means by which he had unraveled them.

"I confess," said he, "that any theories which I had formed from the newspaper reports were entirely erroneous. And yet there were indications there, had they not been overlaid by other details which concealed their true import. I went to Devonshire with the conviction that Fitzroy Simpson was the true culprit, although, of course, I saw that the evidence against him was by no means complete. It was while I was in the carriage, just as we reached the trainer's house, that the immense significance of the curried mutton occurred to me. You may remember that I was distrait and remained sitting after you had all alighted. I was marveling in my own mind how I could possibly have overlooked so obvious a clue."

"I confess," said the colonel, "that even now I cannot see how it helps us."

"It was the first link in my chain of reasoning. Powdered opium is by no means tasteless. The flavor is not disagreeable, but it is perceptible. Were it mixed with any ordinary dish the eater would undoubtedly detect it and would probably eat no more. A curry was exactly the medium which would disguise this taste. By no possible supposition could this stranger, Fitzroy Simpson, have caused curry to be served in the trainer's family that night, and it is surely too monstrous a coincidence to suppose that he happened to come along with powdered opium upon the very night when a dish happened to be served which would disguise the flavor. That is unthinkable. Therefore Simpson becomes eliminated from the case, and our attention centers upon Straker and his wife, the only two people who could have chosen curried mutton for supper that night. The opium was added after the dish was set aside for the stable boy, for the others had the same for supper with no ill effects. Which of them, then, had access to that dish without the maid seeing them?

"Before deciding that question I had grasped the significance of the silence of the dog, for one true inference invariably suggests others. The Simpson incident had shown me that a dog was kept in the stables, and yet, though someone had been in and had fetched out a horse, he had not barked enough to arouse the two lads in the loft. Obviously the midnight visitor was someone whom the dog knew well.

"I was already convinced, or almost convinced, that John Straker went down to the stables in the dead of the night and took out Silver Blaze. For what purpose? For a dishonest one, obviously, or why should he drug his own stable boy? And yet I was at a loss to know why. There have been cases before now where trainers have made sure of great sums of money by laying against their own horses through agents and then preventing them from winning by fraud. Sometimes it is a pulling jockey. Sometimes it is some surer and subtler means. What was it here? I hoped the contents of his pockets might help me form a conclusion.

"And they did so. You cannot have forgotten the singular knife which was found in the dead man's hand, a knife which certainly no sane man would choose for a weapon. It was, as Dr. Watson told us, a form of knife which is used for the most delicate operations known in surgery. And it was to be used for a delicate operation that night. You must know, with your wide experience of turf matters, Colonel Ross, that it is possible to make a slight nick upon the tendons of a horse's ham, and to do it subcutaneously, so as to leave absolutely no trace. A horse so treated would develop a slight lameness, which would be put down to a strain in exercise or a touch of rheumatism, but never to foul play."

"Villain! Scoundrel!" cried the colonel.

"We have here the explanation of why John Straker wished to take the horse out onto the moor. So spirited a creature would have certainly roused the soundest of sleepers when it felt the prick of the knife. It was absolutely necessary to do it in the open air."

"I have been blind!" cried the colonel. "Of course that was why he needed the candle and struck the match."

"Undoubtedly. But in examining his belongings, I was fortunate enough to discover not only the method of the crime but even its motives. As a man of the world, Colonel, you know that men do not carry other people's bills about in their pockets. We have most of us quite enough to do to settle our own. I at once concluded that Straker was leading a double life and keeping a second establishment. The nature of the bill showed that there was a lady in the case, and one who had expensive tastes. Liberal as you are with your servants, one can hardly expect that they can buy twenty-guinea walking dresses for their ladies. I questioned Mrs. Straker as to the dress without her knowing it, and, having satisfied myself that it had never reached her, I made a note of the milliner's address and felt that by calling there with Straker's photograph I could easily dispose of the mythical Derbyshire.

"From that time on all was plain. Straker had led out the horse to a hollow where his light would be invisible. Simpson, in his flight, had dropped his cravat, and Straker had picked it up—with some idea, perhaps, that he might use it in securing the horse's leg. Once in the hollow, he had got behind the horse and had struck a light; but the creature, frightened at the sudden glare, and with the strange instinct of animals feeling that some mischief was intended, had lashed out, and the steel shoe had struck Straker full on the forehead. He had already, in spite of the rain, taken off his overcoat in order to do his delicate task, and so, as he fell, his knife gashed his thigh. Do I make it clear?"

"Wonderful!" cried the colonel. "Wonderful! You might have been there!"

"My final shot was, I confess, a very long one. It struck me that so astute a man as Straker would not undertake this delicate tendon-nicking without a little practice. What could he practice on? My eyes fell upon the sheep, and I asked a question which, rather to my surprise, showed that my surmise was correct.

"When I returned to London I called upon the milliner, who had recognized Straker as an excellent customer of the name of Derbyshire, who had a very dashing wife with a strong partiality for expensive dresses. I have no doubt that this woman had plunged him over head and ears in debt, and so led him into this miserable plot."

"You have explained all but one thing," cried the colonel. "Where was the horse?"

"Ah, it bolted and was cared for by one of your neighbors. We must have an amnesty in that direction, I think. This is Clapham Junction, if I am not mistaken, and we shall be in Victoria in less than ten minutes. If you care to smoke a cigar in our rooms, Colonel, I shall be happy to give you any other details which might interest you."

THE NINE-MILE WALK

Harry Kemelman

I HAD MADE an ass of myself in a speech I had given at the Good Government Association dinner, and Nicky Welt had cornered me at breakfast at the Blue Moon, where we both ate occasionally, for the pleasure of rubbing it in. I had made the mistake of departing from my prepared speech to criticize a statement my predecessor in the office of district attorney had made to the press. I had drawn a number of inferences from his statement and had thus left myself open to a rebuttal which he had promptly made and which had the effect of making me appear intellectually dishonest. I was new to this political game, having but a few months before left the Law School faculty to become the Reform Party candidate for district attorney. I said as much in extenuation, but Nicholas Welt, who could never drop his pedagogical manner (he was Snowdon Professor of English Language and Literature), replied in much the same tone that he would dismiss a request from a sophomore for an extension on a term paper, "That's no excuse."

Although he is only two or three years older than I, in his late forties, he always treats me like a schoolmaster hectoring a stupid pupil. And I, perhaps because he looks so much older with his white hair and lined, gnomelike face, suffer it.

"They were perfectly logical inferences," I pleaded.

"My dear boy," he purred, "although human intercourse is well-nigh impossible without inference, most inferences are usually wrong. The percentage of error is particularly high in the legal profession, where the intention is not to discover what the speaker wishes to convey, but rather what he wishes to conceal."

I picked up my check and eased out from behind the table.

"I suppose you are referring to cross-examination of witnesses in court. Well, there's always an opposing counsel who will object if the inference is illogical."

"Who said anything about logic?" he retorted. "An inference can be logical and still not be true."

He followed me down the aisle to the cashier's booth. I paid my check and waited impatiently while he searched in an old-fashioned change purse, fishing out coins one by one and placing them on the counter beside his check, only to discover that the total was insufficient. He slid them back into his purse and with a tiny sigh extracted a bill from another compartment of the purse and handed it to the cashier.

"Give me any sentence of ten or twelve words," he said, "and I'll build you a logical chain of inferences that you never dreamed of when you framed the sentence."

Other customers were coming in, and since the

space in front of the cashier's booth was small, I decided to wait outside until Nicky completed his transaction with the cashier. I remember being mildly amused at the idea that he probably thought I was still at his elbow and was going right ahead with his discourse.

When he joined me on the sidewalk I said, "A nine-mile walk is no joke, especially in the rain."

"No, I shouldn't think it would be," he agreed absently. Then he stopped in his stride and looked at me sharply. "What the devil are you talking about?"

"It's a sentence and it has eleven words," I insisted. And I repeated the sentence, ticking off the words on my fingers.

"What about it?"

"You said that given a sentence of ten or twelve words—"

"Oh, yes." He looked at me suspiciously. "Where did you get it?"

"It just popped into my head. Come on, now, build your inferences."

"You're serious about this?" he asked, his little blue eyes glittering with amusement. "You really want me to?"

It was just like him to issue a challenge and then to appear amused when I accepted it. And it made me angry.

"Put up or shut up," I said.

"All right," he said mildly. "No need to be huffy. I'll play. Hm-m, let me see, how did the sentence go? 'A nine-mile walk is no joke, especially in the rain.' Not much to go on there."

"It's more than ten words," I rejoined.

"Very well." His voice became crisp as he mentally squared off to the problem. "First inference: The speaker is aggrieved."

"I'll grant that," I said, "although it hardly seems to be an inference. It's really implicit in the statement."

He nodded impatiently. "Next inference: The rain was unforeseen, otherwise he would have said, 'A nine-mile walk in the rain is no joke,' instead of using the 'especially' phrase as an afterthought."

"I'll allow that," I said, "although it's pretty obvious."

"First inferences should be obvious," said Nicky tartly.

I let it go at that. He seemed to be floundering and I didn't want to rub it in.

"Next inference: The speaker is not an athlete or an outdoorsman."

"You'll have to explain that one," I said.

"It's the 'especially' phrase again," he said. "The speaker does not say that a nine-mile walk in the rain is no joke, but merely the walk—just the distance, mind you—is no joke. Now, nine miles is not such a terribly long distance. You walk more than half that in eighteen holes of golf—and golf is an old man's game," he added slyly. *I* play golf.

"Well, that would be all right under ordinary circumstances," I said, "but there are other possibilities. The speaker might be a soldier in the jungle, in which case nine miles would be a pretty good hike, rain or no rain."

"Yes," and Nicky was sarcastic, "and the speaker

might be one-legged. For that matter, the speaker might be a graduate student writing a Ph.D. on humor and starting by listing all the things that are not funny. See here, I'll have to make a couple of assumptions before I continue."

"How do you mean?" I asked suspiciously.

"Remember, I'm taking this sentence *in vacuo,* as it were. I don't know who said it or what the occasion was. Normally a sentence belongs in the framework of a situation."

"I see. What assumptions do you want to make?"

"For one thing, I want to assume that the intention was not frivolous, that the speaker is referring to a walk that was actually taken, and that the purpose of the walk was not to win a bet or something of that sort."

"That seems reasonable enough," I said.

"And I also want to assume that the locale of the walk is here."

"You mean here in Fairfield?"

"Not necessarily. I mean in this general section of the country."

"Fair enough."

"Then, if you grant those assumptions, you'll have to accept my last inference that the speaker is no athlete or outdoorsman."

"Well, all right. Go on."

"Then my next inference is that the walk was taken very late at night or very early in the morning—say, between midnight and five or six in the morning."

"How do you figure that one?" I asked.

"Consider the distance—nine miles. We're in a

fairly well populated section. Take any road and you'll find a community of some sort in less than nine miles. Hadley is five miles away, Hadley Falls is seven and a half, Goreton is eleven, but East Goreton is only eight, and you strike East Goreton before you come to Goreton. There is local train service along the Goreton road and bus service along the others. All the highways are pretty well traveled. Would anyone have to walk nine miles in a rain unless it were late at night when no buses or trains were running and when the few automobiles that were out would hesitate to pick up a stranger on the highway?"

"He might not have wanted to be seen," I suggested.

Nicky smiled pityingly. "You think he would be less noticeable trudging along the highway than he would be riding in a public conveyance where everyone is usually absorbed in his newspaper?"

"Well, I won't press the point," I said brusquely.

"Then try this one: He was walking toward a town rather than away from one."

I nodded. "It is more likely, I suppose. If he were in a town, he could probably arrange for some sort of transportation. Is that the basis for your inference?"

"Partly that," said Nicky, "but there is also an inference to be drawn from the distance. Remember, it's a *nine-mile* walk and nine is one of the exact numbers."

"I'm afraid I don't understand."

That exasperated schoolteacher look appeared on Nicky's face again. "Suppose you say, 'I took a ten-mile walk' or 'a hundred-mile drive'; I would assume that you actually walked anywhere from eight to a

173

dozen miles, or that you rode between ninety and a hundred and ten miles. In other words, *ten* and *hundred* are round numbers. You might have walked *exactly* ten miles, or just as likely you might have walked *approximately* ten miles. But when you speak of walking *nine* miles, I have a right to assume that you have named an exact figure. Now, we are far more likely to know the distance of the city from a given point than we are to know the distance of a given point from the city. That is, ask anyone in the city how far out Farmer Brown lives, and if he knows him, he will say, 'Three or four miles.' But ask Farmer Brown how far he lives from the city and he will tell you, 'Three and six-tenths miles—measured it on my speedometer many a time.' "

"It's weak, Nicky," I said.

"But in conjunction with your own suggestion that he could have arranged transportation if he had been in a city—"

"Yes, that would do it," I said. "I'll pass it. Any more?"

"I've just begun to hit my stride," he boasted. "My next inference is that he was going to a definite destination and that he had to be there at a particular time. It was not a case of going off to get help because his car broke down or his wife was going to have a baby or somebody was trying to break into his house."

"Oh, come now," I said, "the car breaking down is really the most likely situation. He could have known the exact distance from having checked the mileage just as he was leaving town."

Nicky shook his head. "Rather than walk nine miles

in the rain, he would have curled up on the backseat and gone to sleep, or at least stayed by his car and tried to flag another motorist. Remember, it's nine miles. What would be the least it would take him to hike it?"

"Four hours," I offered.

He nodded. "Certainly no less, considering the rain. We've agreed that it happened very late at night or very early in the morning. Suppose he had his breakdown at one o'clock in the morning. It would be five o'clock before he would arrive. That's daybreak. You begin to see a lot of cars on the road. The buses start just a little later. In fact, the first buses hit Fairfield around five thirty. Besides, if he were going for help, he would not have to go all the way to town—only as far as the nearest telephone. No, he had a definite appointment, and it was in a town, and it was for some time before five thirty."

"Then why couldn't he have got there earlier and waited?" I asked. "He could have taken the last bus, arrived around one o'clock, and waited until his appointment. He walks nine miles in the rain instead, and you said he was no athlete."

We had arrived at the Municipal Building, where my office is. Normally any arguments begun at the Blue Moon ended at the entrance to the Municipal Building. But I was interested in Nicky's demonstration, and I suggested that he come up for a few minutes.

When we were seated I said, "How about it, Nicky, why couldn't he have arrived early and waited?"

"He could have," Nicky retorted. "But since he did

175

not, we must assume that he was either detained until after the last bus left, or that he had to wait where he was for a signal of some sort, perhaps a telephone call."

"Then, according to you, he had an appointment sometime between midnight and five thirty—"

"We can draw it much finer than that. Remember, it takes him four hours to walk the distance. The last bus stops at twelve thirty A.M. If he doesn't take that, but starts at the same time, he won't arrive at his destination until four thirty. On the other hand, if he takes the first bus in the morning, he will arrive around five thirty. That would mean that his appointment was for sometime between four thirty and five thirty."

"You mean that if his appointment were earlier than four thirty, he would have taken the last night bus, and if it were later than five thirty, he would have taken the first morning bus?"

"Precisely. And another thing: If he were waiting for a signal or a phone call, it must have come not much later than one o'clock."

"Yes, I see that," I said. "If his appointment is around five o'clock and it takes him four hours to walk the distance, he'd have to start around one."

He nodded, silent and thoughtful. For some queer reason I could not explain, I did not feel like interrupting his thoughts. On the wall was a large map of the county and I walked over to it and began to study it.

"You're right, Nicky," I remarked over my shoulder, "there's no place as far as nine miles away from Fairfield that doesn't hit another town first. Fairfield is right in the middle of a bunch of smaller towns."

He joined me at the map. "It doesn't have to be Fairfield, you know," he said quietly. "It was probably one of the outlying towns he had to reach. Try Hadley."

"Why Hadley? What would anyone want in Hadley at five o'clock in the morning?"

"The Washington Flyer stops there to take on water about that time," he said quietly.

"That's right, too," I said. "I've heard that train many a night when I couldn't sleep. I'd hear it pulling in and then a minute or two later I'd hear the clock on the Methodist church banging out five." I went back to my desk for a timetable. "The Flyer leaves Washington at twelve forty-seven A.M. and gets into Boston at eight A.M."

Nicky was still at the map measuring distances with a pencil.

"Exactly nine miles from Hadley is the Old Sumter Inn," he announced.

"Old Sumter Inn," I echoed. "But that upsets the whole theory. You can arrange for transportation there as easily as you can in a town."

He shook his head. "The cars are kept in an enclosure and you have to get an attendant to check you through the gate. The attendant would remember anyone taking out his car at a strange hour. It's a pretty conservative place. He could have waited in his room until he got a call from Washington about someone on the Flyer—maybe the number of the car and the berth. Then he could just slip out of the hotel and walk to Hadley."

I stared at him, hypnotized.

"It wouldn't be difficult to slip aboard while the train was taking on water, and then if he knew the car number and the berth—"

"Nicky," I said portentously, "as the reform district attorney who campaigned on an economy program, I am going to waste the taxpayers' money and call Boston long distance. It's ridiculous; it's insane—but I'm going to do it!"

His little blue eyes glittered and he moistened his lips with the tip of his tongue.

"Go ahead," he said hoarsely.

I replaced the telephone in its cradle.

"Nicky," I said, "this is probably the most remarkable coincidence in the history of criminal investigation: *A man was found murdered in his berth on last night's twelve forty-seven from Washington!* He'd been dead about three hours, which would make it exactly right for Hadley."

"I thought it was something like that," said Nicky. "But you're wrong about its being a coincidence. It can't be. Where did you get that sentence?"

"It was just a sentence. It simply popped into my head."

"It couldn't have! It's not the sort of sentence that pops into one's head. If you had taught composition as long as I have, you'd know that when you ask someone for a sentence of ten words or so, you get an ordinary statement such as 'I like milk'—with the other words made up by a modifying clause like, 'because it is good for my health.' The sentence you offered related to a *particular situation.*"

"But I tell you I talked to no one this morning. And I was alone with you at the Blue Moon."

"You weren't with me all the time I paid my check," he said sharply. "Did you meet anyone while you were waiting on the sidewalk for me to come out of the Blue Moon?"

I shook my head. "I was outside for less than a minute before you joined me. You see, a couple of men came in while you were digging out your change and one of them bumped me, as I thought I'd wait—"

"Did you ever see them before?"

"Who?"

"The two men who came in," he said, the note of exasperation creeping into his voice again.

"Why, no—they weren't anyone I knew."

"Were they talking?"

"I guess so. Yes, they were. Quite absorbed in their conversation, as a matter of fact—otherwise they would have noticed me and I would not have been bumped."

"Not many strangers come into the Blue Moon," he remarked.

"Do you think it was they?" I asked eagerly. "I think I'd know them again if I saw them."

Nicky's eyes narrowed. "It's possible. There had to be two—one to trail the victim in Washington and ascertain his berth number, the other to wait here and do the job. The Washington man would be likely to come down here afterward. If there were theft as well as murder, it would be to divide the spoils. If it were just murder, he would probably have to come down to pay off his confederate."

I reached for the telephone.

"We've been gone less than half an hour," Nicky went on. "They were just coming in, and service is slow at the Blue Moon. The one who walked all the way to Hadley must certainly be hungry and the other probably drove all night from Washington."

"Call me immediately if you make an arrest," I said into the phone and hung up.

Neither of us spoke a word while we waited. We paced the floor, avoiding each other almost as though we had done something we were ashamed of.

The telephone rang at last. I picked it up and listened. Then I said, "Okay," and turned to Nicky.

"One of them tried to escape through the kitchen, but Winn had someone stationed at the back and they got him."

"That would seem to prove it," said Nicky with a frosty little smile.

I nodded agreement.

He glanced at his watch. "Gracious," he exclaimed, "I wanted to make an early start on my work this morning, and here I've already wasted all this time talking with you."

I let him get to the door. "Oh, Nicky," I called, "what was it you set out to prove?"

"That a chain of inferences could be logical and still not be true," he said.

"Oh."

"What are you laughing at?" he asked snappishly. And then he laughed, too.

THE MAN IN THE VELVET HAT

Jerome and Harold Prince

> This unusual story, because of its experimental style, requires an introduction. The authors, a brother team, combine an unconventional style of punctuation with the motion-picture technique of crosscutting to create a rapid, urgent pace. You'll not soon forget "The Man in the Velvet Hat."

THERE WERE NO searchlights that night. Far down at one end of the corridor, black, no moonlight through the long, open windows, voices, low then loud, slipped through the concrete from the office behind the walls, loud then low, a mumble, a chatter, a senility of sounds. Then a block of light crashed into the hallway —the door of the office was swinging back—and the sounds became laughter, voices, a clarinet's tune— *Come on along, Come on along, Alexander's Ragtime*

Band—and the doorknob cracked hard against a retaining wall. Shadows, three-dimensional, bulged into the doorway; the block of light was veined with moving strata of black, of gray—*It's the best band in the land*—someone, soprano, was singing; voices were hiccoughing, saying good-bye, merry Christmas, good-bye, merry Christmas, good-bye, good-bye. Good-bye, a deep voice answered, good-bye, good-bye, good-bye—*played in ragtime, Come on along, Come on along, Alexander's Ragtime Band*—merry Christmas. Then the shadows stumbled back from the doorway; the man, alone in the corridor, the light upon him, wobbled, grinned, wiped lipstick from his face, straightened his tie, his hat. The office door clicked shut. There was no light now, and only a whispered jazz tune growing fainter; and the man's footsteps sounded loud as they moved up the corridor, sounded louder as they moved more rapidly, seemed one burst of noise as the man began to run. And then there was no sound at all.

When the police found his body in the alley two hours later, there was something ugly where his head had been. The short investigation that followed was decisive. Within an hour the police had learned that the dead man was a boiler salesman, John Mongon; that he was twenty-six years old, had no enemies; and that his death could not possibly have resulted from foul play. Both the plainclothesmen assigned to the case and the local uniformed officer agreed that Mongon, drunk, or at least strongly under the influence of liquor, had left his company's Christmas party at 11:00 P.M. on Monday, December 17, during the height of

183

a practice blackout; that, unable to find his way in the dark, he had walked by the elevator shaft, and then somehow had slipped and plunged through an open casement window. It was death by accident, and so far as the police were concerned the case was closed, despite the morning mail which brought the same letter to Magruder as it did to Reynolds.

Magruder probably never saw the letter that day— it must have been pigeonholed by that clerical machine which is efficient because it has learned not to discriminate—or, if he did see the letter, he had seen so many like it in his long career as a police official that he must have returned it summarily for the clerical machine to pigeonhole. But Reynolds had to see the letter; he had to read it; it was his job. For years now, as a feature writer of that New York daily, as a contributor to the smartest of the slick magazines, he had made a reputation by describing, as Stevenson and Arthur Machen had once done, the romance lurking just beyond the pavement: the unusual, the macabre which rubbed elbows with you in the Polo Grounds, on the B.M.T., along the Bowery, in the middle of Central Park. His early works—he was very young then—were brilliant fantasies, derivatives of James Stephens, Lord Dunsany, Charles Fort, with, if you can imagine it, a strong dose of Ben Hecht and a good deal of O. Henry. But as he and his bank account grew fatter, the rigid discipline which is necessary for the creation of the unreality which is real was, after a small struggle, forgotten, and his poetry became facts, his dreams, articles. People had come to him— all sorts of queer people—telling him queer tales; and letters, from Massillon, Ohio, and others with strange stamps and stranger script had brought the *outré* into his study. Most of those yarns—the identity of Hitler's wife, the man who was Crater, the route to Shangri-La —were, Reynolds had found, amateurish and scarcely original lies; but he had been surprised to learn that some of the stories were true, and he had been even more surprised to learn that the publication of these stories, whether true or not, earned him more money than he had ever made before. It became his practice thereafter to listen closely to his visitors, to read his mail carefully, and, whenever something interested him, to place a large red crayon check on the relevant documents; and sometimes he would investigate these documents before publication, and sometimes he would not.

Check. *My dear Mr. Reynolds, It was My whim two hours ago to take home with Me to Eternity My son, known in this life as John Mongon.* Monday, December 18. It was postmarked 1:00 A.M.

Check. *My dear Mr. Reynolds, In a swift chariot, I have taken Edward Tucker home to Glory.* Tuesday, December 19.

Check. *My dear Mr. Reynolds, Five have been purified by flames and are at peace within My heart.* Wednesday, December 20.

Check. *My dear Mr. Reynolds, I have said love little children, and so I have taken her from suffering to Eternal Happiness.* Thursday, December 21.

Check. *My dear Mr. Reynolds, Let he who is without sin cast the first stone, so she, too, now knows her God.* Friday, December 22.

Check. *My dear Mr. Reynolds, I saw Peter Savitcky today and I knew he was a good man. Peter Savitcky is no longer with you, but with Me in Celestial Happiness; and you must not, John Reynolds, hope that I shall come for you, for I have not willed it, and your time is not yet come. Nor will I be pleased if you seek Me out, even though you cannot. You cannot find Me, John Reynolds, and do not ask your police to help you. They find criminals, John Reynolds—here they must find a crime.* By special delivery, Saturday, December 23.

Check. *And on the Seventh Day He rested.* By telegram, Sunday, December 24.

It was with the arrival of the seventh message on Christmas Eve that the events crystallized for Reynolds —and this he reported later—into a Mendeleev chart of crime, with gaps in the future for events that must occur, with gaps in the past for events that had occurred but had not been observed. It was then that he decided to investigate the incidents of the last week and to find the unknown that he knew must exist. He acted immediately. A telephone call to the office of Western Union brought him no results: The telegram had been dictated from a pay station in the Borough Hall section of Brooklyn; yes, it was a man; no, I couldn't identify the voice; yes, I'm sure. Another call to the local police station wasted a nickel. And the woman who answered the telephone at Magruder's apartment was polite, but nothing could make her admit Magruder was at home. Reynolds dialed another number.

Then, without shaving: from lounging pajamas into

tweed, a camel's hair coat, the Hudson on his left, cold wind against his cheeks, the lights of George Washington Bridge growing nearer, behind him now, the screech of his tires on dirty snow, snowflakes on his collar as he stepped from the car. The man was waiting for him, wanting to hear more; but when he heard what Reynolds had to say, he laughed quietly; and when Reynolds continued, excited now, insisting, the man was impatient; and when Reynolds began to argue, his red hair falling over his eyes, constantly being brushed back with a ticlike gesture, the man said, "Listen, mister, I don't know if you are who you say you are, and I don't care. But get this straight. Peter Savitcky was my brother. If anybody knows anything about him, I know, and I'm telling you this for the last time: My brother died of pneumonia and nothing else."

Then the car again, down a Broadway slippery with ice, across town, under an El, over car tracks and cobblestones, dark tenements on both sides of him, then a small brownstone house, shades pulled down on the windows, stained curtains over a large glass door. She answered the bell——her kimono was clinging tightly to her body——"What you want, white man?" she said; and Reynolds talked, as he had to Peter Savitcky's brother, as he knew he must talk; but she just laughed, "Ain't worth worrying about, mister," she said; and when Reynolds muttered something in a low voice, "I ain't afraid. She was a no-good woman and she got what was coming to her. I saw the streetcar cut her in two, and it was nobody's fault but her own. I swear to God"——she kissed the tip of her small finger and held it high in the air—"I swear to God."

He walked now, a few blocks south to a four-story building of the old type. There was black crepe, already dirty and torn, hanging in the vestibule; the stairs were rotten; insects scurried across the walls; there was black crepe—dirty, too, and torn—hanging on a wooden door two flights up. Inside, it was cold: There was no steam, no stove. An old woman sat on a wooden box, staring in front of her, moaning softly. When Reynolds spoke to her she whimpered. A neighbor said, "Don't. She's almost out of her mind"; and when Reynolds turned to him, questioning, "You're crazy. Her grandmother told her to stay off the ice. A six-year-old girl don't listen. And what could an old lady do?"

He drove across town again, then down the highway, the snow falling more heavily now, the East River dull white, the sound of his tires a soporific crunch; then slush under his wheels as he turned back into the city, pushcarts, delicatessens, slums, a thin red house, skeletal, charred, and a fireman bending his face down to the car window, talking rapidly, and Reynolds answering, arguing, trying to win his point by logic, curses, until the fireman laughed and Reynolds heard him say what the others had said. "But don't you understand," Reynolds still insisted, "that a man smoking in bed could *not* have caused this fire"; but the fireman only smiled. "I don't know anything about that," he said. "Maybe the five guys who were toasted in this little barbecue could tell you more"; and Reynolds shifted gears, cried, "Merry Christmas."

If he were to have continued his journey back into

time, his next stop would have been the Coliseum in the Bronx; but the case of Edward Tucker, who had made his living driving midget racing cars and who had met his death in one, was more blatantly accidental than any of the others; and, besides, it was now nearly eleven. Instead Reynolds drove west, stopping at a drugstore near Fulton Street and Broadway. He waited until a phone booth cleared, then spoke into the mouthpiece for several minutes. When he came out he was sweating, and the night air made him shudder, but he walked up the block to the bookstore on the corner, slumped, tired, against the wall of the building, waited. In five minutes a boy-sized young man wearing an incipient moustache of indeterminate color—pants pegged tightly about his ankles, topcoat hugging his waist, mushrooming widely over his shoulders, low-crowned, all-brim hat perching on the back of his head—approached Reynolds uneasily, finally held out his hand.

"Mr. Reynolds? I'm Larry."

Reynolds took his hand, made the customary remarks, then spoke rapidly.

"Gee, no, Mr. Reynolds. Gee whiz, no!"

For the next few minutes, his back turned to Larry, Reynolds read a hundred titles in the bookstore window and remembered none; then, facing Larry again, he said quietly, "Larry, this is more important to you than it is to me or anybody else. Tell me, on the night Mongon fell through the window did you take anybody up to the party who didn't belong there?"

"No, sir."

"Larry, are you sure?"

"Sure, I'm sure."

"Now, listen, Larry, you know who I am, don't you? That's right. I can make you a pretty famous fellow, Larry—your picture in the paper, everybody talking about you—if you can remember what you saw last Monday night."

"I don't get you, Mr. Reynolds. I told you I saw nobody else."

"Are you sure, Larry? Could you swear to it if you had to in court—particularly if somebody else knew you were mistaken? Larry, our memories are curious things; they play us tricks. Larry, try to remember if you brought anybody else up in the elevator that night—somebody you never saw before."

"Mr. Reynolds, you got me all mixed up. I don't know what you mean."

"Larry! You know what I mean. Oh, all right, we'll pay you fifty dollars for your story. Now, tell me, what happened when you saw him?"

Larry said, "Maybe you mean the tall guy who came in at a quarter to eleven?"

Reynolds said, "Of course. Now, let's have it."

Larry moistened his lips.

"He comes in—it's pretty late. I say, 'Floor, please?' He says, 'Twelve.' I say, 'There ain't nobody on twelve.' He don't say a word. I say, 'The party's on sixteen.' He just ignores me. So I take him up."

"You never saw him before?"

"Never."

"Now, what did he look like, besides being tall?"

"You got me there, Mr. Reynolds. I—"

"You must have seen his face. That's a pretty bright

light in your elevator. Unless . . . he had his hat pulled down so you couldn't see his face. Was that it, Larry? Did he have his hat pulled down over his face?"

"Sure. That's what it was. He had his hat pulled down over his face."

"What kind of hat was it?"

"Black."

"Black? That's all?"

"Well, an ordinary hat. Old, though. Fuzzy."

"Fuzzy? Like old velvet?"

"If you say so."

"Not if I say so. Was it?"

"Okay, Mr. Reynolds, okay. It was like you say—velvet. He wore a raincoat," Larry added.

"Good. What color?"

"Pretty dark. Brown. Dark brown."

"That's fine, Larry. Now, one thing more, and be very careful that you remember this properly: What time did he come down?"

Larry's face was expressionless.

"He never did come down," he said.

Reynolds opened his wallet.

The remainder of that night was, as Reynolds reported it, an adventure in Freudian psychology: an attempt to restore to the consciousness the memory of the man in the velvet hat which was lost in the hinterland of many minds. (*Now, relax, Bessie. Put your head back on the pillow. Close your eyes—and talk, Bessie. Talk about anything that comes into your mind, Bessie, anything at all. How she walked, Bessie. How she walked when the streetcar hit her. Anything, Bessie, anything that comes into your mind.* a tall man black *Anything, Bessie, no matter how small it is, no matter how silly it sounds.* velvet raincoat a tall man black *No matter how silly it sounds, Savitcky, let me know.* a tall man a velvet hat *No matter how silly.* tall black a velvet hat *Here, grandmother, let me fix the pillow under your head. Just relax, rest, rest, rest.* tall black a velvet hat *Rest.* atallmana-brownraincoatavelvethat *Head back on the pillow.* abrownraincoatavelvet *Slowly. Slowly.* atallmanatall-atallmanabrownraincoat in a velvet hat. . . . *A dozen people have sworn that they saw this man talking to the doctor during your brother's crisis. Savitcky, I don't care one way or another, but the police are going to be mighty unpleasant if you deny that you saw him. That suits me, Bessie, but I don't have to remind you that the police and my newspaper might be interested in the business you do. A hundred dollars now—the rest, grandmother, when you find that picture of your daughter. The others swore that they saw this man— surely you're not going to be the only exception?)* And by the morning of Christmas day Reynolds had in his possession the written testimony of seven witnesses; and by the evening of Christmas day, he said later, he had completed his pattern and had finished what was to be the first of a series of articles.

In that story which appeared early on the afternoon of December 26 Reynolds sketched the death scenes of the eight men, the woman, the child, introduced the contents of the letters, stressing the apparent God-substitution schizophrenia, and then made it impossible for the reader to doubt the existence of some agency behind each of the noncriminal acts. How he had searched for that agency and how he had finally identified it as the man in the black velvet hat, he then told in a sequence of exclamation points, culminating in an accusation of murder. "But if murder has been done, and if this man is a murderer"—and now Reynolds was writing as he had a hundred times before— "he is a murderer such as the world has never known, or, perhaps, such as the world has always known, but never seen. There is no motive for any of his crimes, no evidence of lust or of envy, of passion or of gain. He kills by caprice, through kindness, by whim, or by some deep underlying necessity. Certainly if this man is not a God, he has not only successfully adopted the posturings of one, but the psychic attributes as well. Where he walks, death walks—and this man may be Death himself."

There was no comment on the yarn from Magruder, nothing about it in the later editions of the other evening papers, just a casual reference to it by an obscure radio newscaster; but dozens of people came to see Reynolds, others telegraphed or telephoned, and each swore that he had seen the man in the black velvet hat just before or just after a death by accident or by suicide or by disease. Reynolds remembered particularly an old Italian woman—her face was a tangle of hard gray threads—who crossed herself as she talked about her son: dying slowly, screams clinging to the house, the Blessed Saint and prayer, kissing a silver crucifix as she talked, prayer on bony knees in damp churches, again and again and again, then convalescence in the sunlight, laughter in the sunlight, a blanket over his knees, gay in a wheelchair, laughing,

she laughing, too, then a tall man walking in the sunlight, a brown raincoat close to his rib-thin body, a
black velvet hat pulled down hard over his eyes, we,
laughing in the sunlight, Holy Mother, how we laughed
in the sunlight, a lean shadow down the street, a lean
shadow falling on her son, a silent passing—she kissed
the crucifix again—and death. Others remembered
that story, too: it was dramatized on several radio
news programs almost immediately after its publication under Reynolds' byline; it appeared, rewritten,
in several current news magazines, in every paper in
New York; it served to introduce the man in the
black velvet hat to seven million New Yorkers and
to create, if nothing else, a sense of expectation which
was the prelude to the change which came over the
city after the eighth letter was made public on Thursday night.

My dear Mr. Reynolds, it read, *Do not deceive yourself. I have been silent, but I have not rested, nor have
I ever rested. I shall continue to choose as I have always chosen, as the whim strikes me; and as the whim
strikes me, so shall I tell. You will not always know,
John Reynolds, how merciful I have been.*

On the following morning many newspapers began
the practice of publishing a daily list of accidental—
they printed it "accidental"—deaths in a black-lined
box on their front pages; but there was, apparently,
no excitement, except in the voices of radio announc-
ers; no panic, except for those few who had seen the
man in the velvet hat; no fear, except for the quasi-
supernatural warnings of Reynolds and the para-
phrases of his colleagues. New York seemed to go

about its affairs with its customary indifference, but on that Friday night business began to boom in the night clubs, and flop shows dusted off the standing-room-only signs. The Broadway area during the next few days was so crowded that it often took an hour to walk from Fifty-ninth to Forty-second Street. At the Stork Club, at the Famous Door, at 21, at Fefe's Monte Carlo, more people were turned away in one week than had been admitted in the previous six. Eight new jazz bands were imported: six from Chicago, two from New Orleans. The waiting lines to the larger motion picture houses were often as long as two city blocks. There were no cabs to be had at all in the midtown area. At Macy's, in five other department stores, the Bible topped all book sales. Restaurants placed their chairs back to back, and a local comic added to his act a sketch of Casper Milquetoast trying to drink a brimming glass of milk at Dinty Moore's. But on January 5, all that stopped.

By curtain time of that day four men and two women had already died, and of the six others at the Polyclinic Hospital only two were to survive. Most reporters, including Reynolds, credited the first scream ("I did it to warn the others," she said) to a small upholstered woman of about forty; others placed the blame on a middle-aged male neurasthenic, on an unemployed salesman, on a high-school girl. But the official ' report submitted to Magruder spoke of the cause of the panic as a simultaneity of shouts and screams and of the impossible task of fixing respon-sibility on any known person: By the time the police had arrived, there was no trace of the man in the velvet hat, and no one had seen him enter the Radio Building, and no one had seen him leave. But more than two hundred people of the studio audience swore that they had rushed by him just after the first screams —and all New York knew that Reynolds must have received that ninth letter, even though he did not publish it. His column of the next day, denying receipt of the letter, stridently proving—and this was not at all in Reynolds' style—that there could be no connection between the incidents at the radio station and the man in the velvet hat was met by New York with the same cynicism with which it meets all mollifying propaganda—and it was after that, late on Sunday night, that Reynolds and Magruder came face-to-face for the first time.

They sat opposite each other, across a small round table, lamplight hushing the ugliness of the room, steam hissing fitfully from a radiator, an old electric clock wheezing, ticking loudly, Reynolds, Magruder, watching each other, listening to the mayor's footsteps as he walked on the thinly carpeted floor, Magruder a bludgeon, a roll of fat curving over the mayor's high white stiff collar like a half-baked doughnut, walking, Reynolds sweating, the mayor talking on and on, pacing up and down, Magruder's eyes hard on Reynolds, on and on, Magruder *Listen, Reynolds, I've been a policeman for forty years. I've seen them come and go. Tricks don't fool me.* The mayor, across the room, his hands behind his back, mop of hair in his eyes, shouting, walking, his hands on the table now, his face close to theirs, walking again, Magruder saying nothing, Reynolds blinking the sting of a sweat drop from his eye, Magruder *I've walked beats on nights so cold that fat body of yours would have shriveled. I have a bullet buried somewhere in my chest.* The steam screeching from the radiator, the mayor's words drowned in it, weather strips along the windows, fog liquefying against the panes, the mayor smashing his pudgy fist on the table, asking a question, quiet now.

"Maybe there isn't any murderer," Magruder said. "Not in the ordinary sense."

Reynolds tried to say, then said, "I believe there is."

Magruder went on talking. "The letters that Reynolds got came to us, too. You know that. We checked each one—different typewriter, different stationery, no fingerprints. I don't know if one man wrote them. Or, if he did, he's the cleverest crank I've ever come across. And even if it is the work of one man, there's nothing to connect the writer of the letters with murder. Except for that little picnic at the radio station, every death was accidental or natural as sure as we three are in this room."

The mayor dragged a small armchair from a corner of the room, forced himself into it, formed a triangle around the table. The clock was ticking more loudly than ever.

Magruder said, "I'd like to put the screws on some of those people who saw the man in the velvet hat. I'd like to bet he'd disappear just like—" He snapped his fingers.

Reynolds stood up. The perspiration on his body had turned cold. The mayor talked directly to Magruder.

"Forget it." His shrill voice was always pitched to a key of anger. It hid, perhaps, what may have been other emotional states. "You couldn't prove it if you had until doomsday to do it, and if you did no one would believe you. To them, the man in the velvet hat is real, and there's panic."

Magruder lit his pipe, blew out the match. "That's not so. Not in New York. There never will be panic in New York."

"Magruder! Magruder, you think a panic is what happened at the radio station. Somebody screams, 'He's here!' and people lose their heads and trample each other to death. You can't imagine the whole city acting like that. I can't either. But a panic in New York is a cold thing. Listen to me. How's show business? Did you ever see Times Square as empty as you did last night? What was the attendance at the basketball carnival? People are avoiding crowds. They won't admit it. They won't even think it, but what happened at the radio station, they're afraid will happen again. And they're just afraid. They're really scared blue, Magruder."

Reynolds sat down, unbuttoned his vest, straightened his tie, then buttoned his vest. He said, "Why don't you catch him?"

The mayor grasped Magruder's coat lapel. "I want to stop all this. Show them that we can stop it—if there is no man in the velvet hat, invent one, and get him."

"That won't help." Reynolds' voice was louder than the ticking of the clock. "He'll murder again. It will be worse."

"I won't do it," said Magruder. "That's not my style."

The mayor drummed with his child-sized fingers on the liquor-stained, coffee-stained surface of the table; Reynolds looked from one to the other, trying to catch an expression on their averted faces; the steam began to hammer and sizzle in the risers. Magruder knocked ashes from his pipe, a dying cinder glowing on the rug.

"The way I see it"—Magruder's tone was speculative, his voice low—"the thing is either a hoax, or there is a man in the velvet hat—perhaps a crank, perhaps a murderer. If we can prove the hoax or catch our man, the panic, such as it is, disappears. I think we can do it—with Reynolds' cooperation. . . . I'm going to challenge the man in the velvet hat—and Reynolds is going to publish that challenge. I'm going to say that I don't think he's a god, and I don't think he's a good criminal. I'm going to say I don't even think he *is* a criminal; anybody can boast of a murder after it's happened, but only a master criminal can boast of a murder before it's happened—and get away with it."

The mayor smiled; his whole face became a series of semicircles curving upward.

"You see the implications," Magruder went on, as slowly as before. "If he doesn't accept the challenge, or if he does accept the challenge and doesn't show up—" He made a gesture indicating finality. "And if he accepts the challenge and tries to succeed, we'll nab him. In either case the thing is done. Can I count on Reynolds' help?"

The mayor said, "Yes."

Reynolds had picked up his hat and cane. He was on his feet, walking to the door. He stopped, turned.

"My own guess is"—he was trying to make himself heard above the banging of the steam, the ticking of the clock—"that he will accept the challenge, and that when he does you will not nab him."

And then it was night again, the Times Building a pale shadow across the street, sounds centrifuged at him, amoeba forms of clouds tasting and disgorging a full white moon, hints of rain slapping his cheeks, jazz from the dance hall overhead, a drunken clown shouting, "Nine o'clock and all's well. Nine o'clock and all's well." *Come on along, Come on along, Alexander's Ragtime Band.* The illuminated dial of his watch told Magruder that it was only three minutes to nine—three more minutes, three minutes to nine. *it's the bestest band what am* Simon and Thompson were in front of the Times Building. Burke and LaMantia were in the lobby. Rowan was across the street on Seventh Avenue. The homicide squad was scattered over the theatrical district. He wanted to, but he didn't dare increase the uniformed police force. No one else knew—only Reynolds, himself, his assistant, Kuchatsky, and the man who wrote the note— written this time in medieval script, delicate colors on yellow parchment. *if you want to hear the Swanee River* Two minutes, two minutes more, two minutes. Anyway, it's over with. After tonight. . . . *At nine o'clock, precisely, on Wednesday night, January 10, a man will die, poisoned, in front of the Times Building. After this I will move again in silence, for only*

201

those without faith need signs. There was a glinting sheet of rain in front of him now. *honey lamb honey lamb* Kuchatsky slipped under the awning, dripping wet, a stream of water running from his hat. We thought we had him, Chief. In front of the Majestic . . . fit the description to a T . . . turned out to be one of our own boys from Staten Island. They laughed. Another minute, one more minute, less now, less than a minute. *Alexander's Ragtime Band*. Keep your eyes open. Cars were sliding on the water-smooth asphalt. The traffic cops cursed. I see by the clock, Chief, that it's nine o'clock. Done. We'll stick around—maybe his watch is slow. They laughed. Another plainclothesman elbowed his way through to the awning. He was sweating, but he was grinning. Overhead they were beginning to jam it, bass fiddle throbbing, traps coughing out hoarse subliminals. A man was standing on the Seventh Avenue curb, watching the cars. *ragtime ragtime ragtime* The man was wearing no hat; he was carrying a coat under his arm. He was watching the sliding cars carefully. *come on come on come on along* A trumpet pleading.

The man leapt. Magruder started forward. The man was avoiding the cars, weaving like a basketball player, running hard. Somebody called him something uncomplimentary. He was running toward the wedge-end of the Times Building, drenched to the skin.

come on along bugle call in the land in the land

The man was more than halfway across. The traffic cop was shouting at him. Magruder was waving at Simon and Thompson in the lobby of the Times Building. They didn't see him. The man's coat in the

dim-out blackness could have been any color, but it was cloth, tweed.

The man had reached the sidewalk in front of the Times Building. There was some light on him. He was tall and thin. He fumbled in his pocket.

It was the clarinet's lick now. He was warming up, playing it straight for a few bars. *it's the best band in the land if you want to hear* The man was raising his hand to his mouth, gulping out of a tiny bottle—and then he began to crumble, liquidly, like a trick shot from a motion picture.

Magruder began to sprint. Kuchatsky blew his whistle. Thompson and Simon were already bending over the man. The others were running, too. The traffic cop was trying to hold off the crowd.

Magruder said, "Take him to a hospital."

Simon said, "He's dead as a doornail."

Then Magruder looked at the man. He knew he had never seen that pain-distorted face before, drops of water pounding on open eyes. He knelt and closed the eyelids. Then he picked up the man's coat, held it in his hand. It was light—too light. He shook it. Oilskin glistened where lining should have been. He turned the coat inside out. It was a raincoat now, and brown. Out of one pocket, crumpled, jutted a black velvet hat.

Kuchatsky tugged at Magruder's sleeve. "Look, Chief. The boys say he dropped it just before he kicked off." Folded vellum, tied with a string; Magruder, automatically untying the string; blocked Gothic letters, in red, in blue, rain covering them with a wavering film—*And God,* it read, *so loved this world that*

He gave His only begotten Son.

Traffic had stopped; there was an excited crowd-whisper all about, but across the street the jazz men were taking a rest. Magruder began to whistle softly. The tune was "Alexander's Ragtime Band."

Then the mayor said, seesawing on the swivel chair behind Magruder's desk, "This is thanks"—winter sunlight breaking against Venetian blinds, the room soft shadows, Magruder leaning under a photograph, Reynolds grinning—"man to man, this is thanks." And Magruder, irritated, playing with the tassels of the blinds, sucking on a long-cold pipe, saying, "Yes, yes, we have a good deal to thank Reynolds for." And Reynolds, easy on the leather lounge, his red hair parted, smooth, the points of his white handkerchief distinct against the brown covert of his suit, bland, happy, saying the proper things— "So, Reynolds, this is thanks, but you surprised me. When he died that way, even *I* thought the thing was supernatural. 'Don't have to give me odds,' I said, 'that Reynolds will play it up for all he's worth and leave us in a worse mess than we were before.' Not surprised?" Magruder's head pivoting in negation.

"Why should you be surprised?" asked Reynolds. "I admit I'd fancy a supernatural ending to a natural one. After all, that's my trade. But when Magruder told me about the suicide—about his being insane, I mean—what could I think? It was clear then that he couldn't have been associated with the crimes in that inexplicable manner I dreamed of. Actually, there were no crimes; he must have attached his mad ego

205

to each death after the fact. How he got the information so quickly, I don't know, but Magruder says it's easy enough. And once he knew, he appeared at or near the scene of the death in that striking costume, and then he posted the letters. That some witnesses swore he appeared before the deaths—well, that's a human failing, isn't it?

"He was a true psychopath; there's no doubt about that. In his own, diseased brain he was a death-dealing but merciful God, taking to rest those who were 'heavy laden' or rewarding the Good of the earth with the joys of Paradise; and even to the end, he was madly consistent, sacrificing himself rather than admit his inability to meet Magruder's challenge. . . . There was no other way to see it—agreed? That's what I wrote."

"It was enough," said the mayor. "It brought us back to normalcy." And Magruder striding to his desk, standing over the mayor. "I have work to do," he said. They, arising, making apologies, the mayor, his back to Magruder, chuckling, the mayor, walking to the door, outside in the corridor, Reynolds still in the room, at the door, the mayor turning to Reynolds, winking, Reynolds adjusting his scarf, the mayor poking Reynolds in the ribs with his elbow, shouting, "Listen, Magruder. Congratulations to you, too. That challenge idea—it was brilliant," laughing silently; and Magruder, head bent over his desk, reports scattered about him, answering softly, "Was it? It amazes me that a hundred lunatics didn't show up, not just one." The mayor, laughing freely now, Magruder head low, footsteps fainter, the glass door closing with a quiver, Magruder busy reading, annotating, scribbling on a small white pad, yawning, stretching, looking up. Reynolds was standing in front of him.

"Yes?"

Staccato: "It was a queer case, Magruder, wasn't it? Not really knowing. . . . All that. . . ."

"Yes?"

"I had the right hunch from the beginning. . . . Kept it to myself, you know. . . . Interesting stud', lunacy. . . ."

"Yes."

"Funny thing, though. About the lunatic, I mean. You never did find out who he really was, did you?"

"Look here, Reynolds, I had you pegged from the start." He turned again to his paper-disarrayed desk.

Reynolds stood where he was. "What do you mean," he asked, " 'pegged from the start'?"

Magruder looked up.

"Interested?"

"Yes."

"Why?"

"I don't know precisely. Curiosity. Was it because you thought I had easy access to the information—my being a newspaperman, I mean?"

"Maybe."

"Do you think I gave the information to the man in the velvet hat?"

"No. . . . I never thought there was a man in the velvet hat. I thought you wrote the letters."

"I? *You* had as easy access to the information as I had. Why didn't *you* write the letters?"

"I had no motive."

"Motive! What motive could I have?"

Magruder said, "I'm an old-fashioned cop, Reynolds, and I always ask, 'Who gains?' You gained—in more ways than one. Do you remember what you wrote after that Orson Welles broadcast? 'If he had done that deliberately,' you said—oh, I don't know if I'm quoting you exactly—you said, 'then it would have been the grimmest but the most satisfactory of literary achievements.' "

"That!"

"Not only that. You had access; you had motive; and it was you who supplied the witnesses and interviewed them before anyone else. It would have been easy for you to have fixed the details of the man in the velvet hat in their minds by coercion, by bribery. . . ."

Magruder said, "Maybe we found the typewriters; maybe we didn't. But if we didn't you can be sure that we will. Maybe I was so sure because I knew beforehand what you'd do after the panic at the radio station. You never could have anticipated the screams of an exhibitionist female—and homicide frightened you. I knew you'd claim there was no letter; I knew you'd deny any connection between the man in the velvet hat and the deaths at the radio station, because the game was getting out of hand, and your wind was up."

Reynolds said, "So that was what you thought."

"That is what I think."

And Reynolds, wiping his face with his pocket handkerchief: "A beautiful theory, Magruder, but spoiled by an ugly fact—" Magruder tilting back in his swivel chair, Reynolds waving good-bye. "There was a man in the velvet hat, Magruder"—Magruder filling his pipe, Reynolds, back to Magruder, walking to the door—"and you have him"—scarf adjusted, hat set right, hand on the doorknob.

Magruder saying, "But we haven't the man in the velvet hat."

And Reynolds stopping, turning on one foot, facing Magruder, Magruder puffing on his pipe, Reynolds walking slowly again toward the desk. "How do you know?" Magruder laughing.

"Because the man we found dead was released from an asylum *only two days before* you published my challenge. He couldn't have been the man in the velvet hat all those other times—not while he was *in* the asylum."

And Reynolds, sober, then frantic, his palms flat on Magruder's desk, his body leaning over the desk, Magruder swinging forward to meet him, Reynolds, Magruder, faces inches apart, Magruder shouting, "You wrote your script. Then you got some poor diseased brain—bribery, coercion, again—to play your principal role."

Reynolds trying to say something, the door opening behind him, a little fat man, perspiring, Kuchatsky, happy, shoving the little man in front of him. Kuchatsky: "Here he is, Chief. From a secondhand typewriter store in Flatbush."

Then Kuchatsky pointing to Reynolds, the secondhand dealer squinting, nodding. "That's him!" Nodding, nodding. "That's the man! That's the man!"

And Reynolds blurting, "Magruder, listen to me.

When I began I never dreamt—"

Magruder spoke slowly. "I talked to the D.A. this morning," he said. "He didn't think we could make a charge of homicide stick. . . . But that was this morning, Reynolds; that was this morning."

Whitman CLASSICS and ANTHOLOGIES

Black Beauty

Little Women

Heidi

Heidi Grows Up

Tom Sawyer

Huckleberry Finn

The Call of the Wild

Treasure Island

Alice in Wonderland

The Wonderful Wizard of Oz

Famous Fairy Tales

Algonquin: The Story of a Great Dog

Tales of Poe

SHORT STORY COLLECTIONS

A Batch of the Best (Stories for Girls)

Like It Is (Stories for Girls)

Shudders

Golden Prize

That's Our Cleo! *(New)*

Way Out *(New)*

Whitman NOVELS FOR GIRLS

Spirit Town

Gypsy From Nowhere

The Family Name

True to You

Practically Twins

Make-Believe Daughter

The Silver Seven

Bicycles North! *(New)*

Whitman ADVENTURE and MYSTERY Books

THE TRIXIE BELDEN SERIES

16 Exciting Titles

MEG MYSTERIES

The Disappearing Diamonds

The Secret of the Witch's Stairway

The Treasure Nobody Saw

The Ghost of Hidden Springs

The Mystery of the Black-Magic Cave

Mystery in Williamsburg

DONNA PARKER

Takes a Giant Step

On Her Own

Mystery at Arawak

Special Agent

KIM ALDRICH MYSTERIES

Miscalculated Risk

Silent Partner

The Deep Six *(New)*

The Long Shot *(New)*

TELEVISION FAVORITES

Lassie
  Lost in the Snow
  Trouble at Panter's Lake

The Mod Squad

Hawaii Five-O

Family Affair

SPORTS AND ADVENTURE STORIES

Throw the Long Bomb! (Football)

Basket Fever (Basketball)

Cellar Team (Baseball)

Drag Strip Danger (Racing)

Divers Down! (Undersea Adventure)

TEE-BO, THE TALKING DOG

2 Titles in This Rollicking New Series